AGAINST THE ODDS

A COLD WAR TALE OF CHOCOLATE, COURAGE, AND LOYALTY BEHIND THE IRON CURTAIN

BERLIN FRACTURED
BOOK FIVE

MARION KUMMEROW

CHAPTER 1

East Berlin, February 1953

"This is not my Berlin," Floriane Eilers thought as she braved the elements, keeping her head down, preferring not to look around where reminders of a terrible time were hideously evident.

It was a bitterly cold day in February and the bad weather only added to her foul mood. The icy wind whipped her coat and scarf about her as she trudged home after a long day at work, careful not to slip on the frozen pavement with its potholes created during the war.

Her steps quickened. It pained her to cross the park, which was still a wasteland after years of promised restoration. The people had long since cut down the trees to use as firewood, leaving behind dead stumps and roots jutting out of the frozen earth like gravestones. But who could blame the living for wanting the warmth the wood would provide?

Flori, as her friends called her, walked past the hills of rubble across the open square, where a vendor greeted her cheerfully from a makeshift stand selling newspapers.

"It's a cold day, isn't it Fräulein?" He stomped about trying to keep warm. "Would you like to buy a paper? The government is about to release the new five-year plan."

"Not today, thank you." Money was tight and she'd rather spend it on food than news she could get for free on the radio tonight. She quickened her pace to get home in time before her younger sister Katja was due to return from high school, from which she was going to graduate with her *Abitur* in a few months' time.

At the tender age of fifteen, Flori had lost her parents and both of her older brothers in the last months of the Second World War. After that it had been only herself and Katja, six years younger than her. Naturally, she had taken on the responsibility of caring for her little sister. Privations, hunger, loss and grief had bound them closely together, although she often felt more like a mother to Katja rather than a sister.

Taking care of Katja and ensuring her education was a serious responsibility. Over the years, circumstances had forced Flori to put her own aspirations aside, and to work tirelessly to keep her little family together.

It had been hard; Flori had sacrificed her education, her dreams of becoming a fashion designer and of having a home and family, to labor in a chocolate factory, earning barely enough to put food on the table, keep a roof over their heads, and send Katja to school. At least her sister would be able to fulfill her dreams, even if Flori could not.

Her sewing helped and she was getting more orders than she had time to meet. She was a master at alterations, such as sprucing up a formerly frumpy frock. She didn't need more than a few scraps of ever-scarce fine fabrics or some strategically placed tucks to create a fashionable dress that, if worn by a pretty young woman, turned heads and evoked whistles everywhere she went. However, it was unfortunate that, after working long shifts at the factory, plus keeping a home where Katja could be happy, Flori didn't have much time or energy left for sewing.

Finally, she arrived at the large building where they had been assigned a one-bedroom apartment in a recently-constructed, large panel-system build. Her sister often complained that it was the size of a postage stamp. Despite the bickering, though, both of them knew they were lucky to live somewhere with a leakproof roof, since there were places much worse in East Berlin. Eight years after the war, people still lived in basements or hastily patched-up ruins. The socialist government simply couldn't construct residential buildings fast enough to make up for the millions of homes destroyed by bombs.

Walking into the kitchen, she kindled the embers in the coal stove and chopped potatoes for a stew. Flori reflected on how much harder the chore of cooking had become since 1948, when the common German energy system had been cut off in an act of retribution by the Imperialist West. The German Democratic Republic had since had to make do with the lesser quality lignite, which was full of water, rather than the hard coal formerly supplied from the Ruhr region.

Even lignite was almost impossible to buy, because most of the production was shipped to their brother country, the Soviet Union, as reparations for the damage sustained during the World War – obviously the West refused to chip in with their share, instead letting the East shoulder all of the burden.

Flori stabbed the knife furiously into a potato. Hadn't everyone suffered enough? Now the imperialists begrudged them any little happiness and tried to suppress the young GDR wherever they could – at least that's what the newspapers always claimed.

After having to leave school at thirteen, due to the war, Flori had never had the chance to receive a higher education and depended entirely on the newspapers or the radio to form her opinion.

She shook her head. It didn't serve her well to dwell on things she couldn't change. Soon enough, Katja would stand on her own two feet, and Flori might finally be able to pursue her own dreams.

She stirred the potato pieces into the pot. For once, she was grateful for the apartment's small size, since the warmth of the kitchen stove spread into the adjacent living room and even into their shared bedroom.

While the stew simmered, she set the mismatched plates on the table. On her way back into the kitchen, she gazed at a picture of herself from before the war. As she took in the golden hair and the chubby cheeks, Flori instinctively ran a hand over her bony shoulders. A sigh escaped her lips. With a bit of time and attention she would be pretty again, but time and money were rare commodities, not to be wasted on frivolities.

A knock on the front door interrupted her reverie. Flori opened it to a visibly agitated Max, who walked right in without a word.

"Hello, Max! Please do come in," she exclaimed with a teasing grin. They were such good friends that they often ignored pleasantries and got straight to the point.

Max Hempel, with whom she'd played in the sandbox, worked with a construction company. Like Flori, he hadn't been able to attend high school or university. However, this did not hold him back. He had an eye for the proportions of buildings the way she intuitively knew how to make the best of an ugly dress. He was a wizard at all things mathematical or technical and, due to hard work combined with brilliance, her childhood friend had recently been promoted to head of his department. The young republic needed people like him.

The construction company that employed Max had built their entire apartment complex of ten towers and, thanks to him putting in a good word, Flori had been able to rent one of the precious spaces in a city starved of accommodation. Small as the flat may be, it nonetheless was an absolute luxury to be comfortably housed during these trying times.

"Katja is not home," Flori said, observing how he his eyes scanned the small living room.

"I wasn't looking for her," Max replied, even as his red face gave him away and he defensively raised his hands in mock surrender.

She had suspected for a few months now that Max, her dearest friend, was sweet on her sister. At first, she'd been scandalized. After all, Katja was her baby sister.

After giving the matter some thought she'd realized she was being over-protective and silly. Katja would turn eighteen within a month; she had grown into an adult woman, and a very pretty one too. It was only natural that she was attracting male attention.

Perhaps it was time to stop seeing her as a little girl who needed protection. A six-year age difference was nothing for a couple and, most importantly, Max was a wonderful man: kind, caring, handsome, and a hard worker. He was destined to get ahead in his construction company and would certainly be able to support a wife and family.

"So, what's up, Max?" she asked, aware of the distress in his face.

"Nothing..." He frowned. "Just work stuff."

He would tell her when he was ready. Having lost his entire family, Max had attached himself to Flori and vice versa. Their strong friendship was a blessing to both of them. They could always rely on each other in times of trouble, no questions asked. Max had often been her only confidante during the difficult post-war years when she'd fought not only for her own survival, but had also gone through the travails of raising a temperamental teenager.

"Do you want to stay for dinner? Katja should be home soon."

Max's face lit up at the mention of her younger sister, confirming her suspicions that he'd fallen in love with Katja. If anything came of it, he'd make a good husband.

Her heart softened. She too, wished for a man in her life. It was never Max, whom she adored in a brotherly way. Theirs was a platonic friendship in the truest sense of the word.

During work, grinding cocoa beans into a thick, smooth paste called chocolate liquor, her mind would often travel to faraway places where she would meet a handsome, mysterious man, who instantly fell in love with her. The fantasy usually ended quickly when the supervisor shouted at her to pay attention to her work and not waste so many beans, or else he would dock her salary.

"I never say no to dinner." Max grinned. "Know what? I'll make myself useful hanging up the bookshelf while you cook."

"That would be great!" Flori grinned as she retreated to the kitchen to stir the stew. Just last week, she'd bought the old bookshelf at a flea market, and hadn't found the time yet to put it into use. Secretly, she'd hoped Max would come over and offer to affix it.

Max was finished in no time at all and sauntered into the kitchen with a much more relaxed expression. Perhaps now he was ready to tell her what bothered him.

"Want a hot chocolate?"

"You have real chocolate?" A wistful grin lit up his handsome, rugged face.

"I happen to have a small amount. We scored a deal with a Dutch company to produce chocolate for them, as long as they provide us with the cocoa beans. I swept up the leftovers and was allowed to bring them home." She worked in the so-called grinder department, where raw materials, and sometimes the hard-to-come-by cocoa beans, were ground into powder and mixed with other ingredients to create the chocolate base for their products.

"Yuk!" Max grimaced.

"Come on. Our factory is spotless; besides, I didn't sweep the floor, just the tables." Flori broke out into giggles. Max's company always relaxed her, because when they spent time together they could just be themselves.

"Sounds awful." He made a wry face supported by an exaggerated shudder.

"If you're this squeamish I better not tell you what we put into the national chocolate." Her hands akimbo, she fixed him with a stare, daring him to ask.

"No need to tell me. I'd rather cling to the idea that Vitalade is real chocolate," he replied, hands clasped in a plea to keep her knowledge to herself.

In the absence of the cocoa needed to make real chocolate, Vitalade was in hot demand as a substitute made mostly of oatmeal, brewing malt, soy flour and hydrogenated vegetable fat.

Extreme shortages after the war had created a whole range of these products. Coffee made from nuts and meat made from beans. Butter was replaced with some curdled concoction while cooking oil was substituted by a mixture of pulped vegetables and spices. It was better not to question the ingredients, if one wanted to eat with gusto.

Flori left Max to add water to the powdered milk, and heat it while carefully stirring in the luxurious chocolate dust. Then she took the hot pot from the stove, inhaling the sweet, slightly bitter aroma with a hint of fruitiness, and poured the steaming liquid into two mugs.

When she returned to the living room, Max was pacing up and down furiously, despite the lack of space hindering his movement. Four steps forward and six steps round the coffee table, which was covered with a cloth to hide its original purpose as a packing crate. A frown creased his brow as he walked, his hands intermittently running through his thick, light-brown hair or balled up into tight fists. There was a disturbed wildness to the man, so unlike the even-tempered, composed person he usually was.

"Sorry." He jumped at the sight of her and sat down heavily on the sofa that was actually a couple of old boxes padded by a quilt and covered by an old sheet. Max had built it, and Flori had given it the cozy look.

She was a homemaker at heart, decorating her apartment into a comfy place despite the shortages of material. Handstitched squares stuffed with summer clothes served as both storage and cushions. Wild flowers, that had dared to bloom on her route from work, found a home in an old bottle serving as a vase. A cracked, old saucer waited to receive ash and cigarette butts. And now the old shelf had found pride of place on the living room wall.

"Here you go." Flori handed him the steaming mug. They had known each other long enough not to waste time on niceties, so she got straight to the point. "What's the problem, Max?"

"The government has increased production quotas again. I mean, we're already breaking our backs building as much as we possibly can, and now they've decided it's not enough and we need to do more." He glared at her almost as if she was to blame, his usually kind brown eyes glittering with suppressed fury.

Flori knew all about increased production quotas, suffering from them herself. Everything was hard to come by in the young German Democratic Republic and the government funneled the scarce materials to where it believed them to be best employed: mostly to heavy industry, partly to the construction business and, to a much lesser extent, food production.

"I know. As if it isn't hard enough to buy the cocoa we need to produce the amounts of end product they want, they then force us to sell the good stuff to the West in exchange for hard currency needed to buy steel and other supplies for the heavy industries." She shook her head in frustration. "Does the government believe the population doesn't need food?"

"It's not fair. We're breaking our backs to rebuild the country and what do the politicians do?" Max scowled and then answered his own question. "Make speeches full of empty promises! Where's the economic upswing? The grand life for all citizens? The fair chances for everyone, independent of their background?"

"Shush!" She nervously looked over her shoulder.

"See! You can't even voice any criticism in your own home out of fear of repercussions. It's like Hitler all over again."

"Please, keep your voice down," she begged her friend. "You of all people should know how thin the walls in this building are. And believe me, they do have ears, too. One of Müller's neighbors reported him for speaking out against corruption and naming names. Within a day the police showed up and took him away."

"You're right. I should know these walls are flimsy." The hard lines around Max's mouth softened into a smile. "I helped build them, after all. And we skimped on material wherever we could."

"Please be serious," Flori pleaded, worried by his rash talk. "Frau Müller is so distraught. I would have comforted her if I hadn't been too afraid to liaise with someone whose husband is deemed a traitor to the country."

Max shrugged, obviously unwilling to discuss this topic. He reached out for his mug and took another sip. "I was so hopeful for a better future. I was convinced we could believe the promises to get ahead by all of us working together to make it happen. All my coworkers in the combinate are willing to give their best." He gave another tired shrug. "Nobody appreciates our work and every small progress is sidelined by the Soviets via their damn reparations."

Flori gasped. Nobody had the right to criticize their brother nation, the first among equals. She quickly added, "They have suffered so much by our hand in the war, it's only just to make up for that as much as we can."

"To the extent of taking our own future away? What utter nonsense!" Max gave a coarse laugh. "Don't you think we could help them better if they let us thrive first, instead of strangling our economy up to a point where we're about to drown?"

"Come on, it's not that bad. There is no way we could hope for a miraculous recovery after all the destruction caused." She put her own mug down, trying to dispel uncomfortable facts by ignoring them. In the past eight years she'd carefully avoided reflecting on the future, since she was too busy merely surviving day-to-day, struggling to keep Katja and herself afloat.

"Keep deluding yourself," Max said. "The cost of living keeps going up. Prices of food, clothing and housing have skyrocketed, while our wages have remained stagnant. It's become increasingly difficult to make ends meet, let alone save up for a rainy day."

She slowly sipped her drink so she could think before she replied. "It's because they divided our city into East and West. It is not just a matter of politics, but of our daily lives. Traveling from one side to the other is a daunting task, with checkpoints and restrictions at every turn."

"Well, and whose fault is that?"

Flori squinted her eyes at him. "The Western Allies', naturally. Marshal Kapralov had to walk out on the Allied Control Council because the American Kommandant of Berlin had treated him with disrespect one time too often." Marshal Kapralov had been the head of the Soviet Military Administration in Germany back then. Following his walkout of the institution governing Berlin, the quadripartite regimen had effectively ceased to exist.

"You don't really believe that, now do you?" Max snorted. "It was simply an excuse, a ploy that enabled Marshal Kapralov, a few weeks later, to block all entry to the Western sectors of Berlin."

Flori wrinkled her nose. "That's not true. The transport controls were needed to counter the flight of capital after the West's currency reform. Which, by the way, they did for the sole purpose of harming our economy."

"That's bullshit and you know it."

Thankfully, a plop from the kitchen relieved her of having to answer. She hurried to stir the stew. Despite always repeating the official line, doubts had been creeping into her mind ever since she had noticed the changes in the political landscape.

Ever so slowly, the unions had turned into the mouthpiece of the government instead of representing the workers, all under the premise that, in a democratic republic, what the government wanted was, by definition, also the will of the people.

Flori had joined the SED party, not because she cared in the least about politics, but because the ruling party controlled all the industries in East Germany. Being a party member had made her eligible for a promotion and a raise in salary, which wasn't awarded to non-party members. Money was always in short supply, because even though school and class books were free, she still had to provide for notebooks, pencils, clothing and whatnot for her sister.

Several minutes later, she called into the living room. "Dinner is ready. I wonder where Katja is? She should have arrived already."

"Do you want to wait for her?" Max's disappointed expression caused her to grin.

"No. She knows what time we eat, so I won't punish a hungry visitor for her unpunctuality."

"Thank God. I'm starving."

Flori grabbed the pot and carried it over to the table, where Max was sitting and waiting for her. For several minutes they ate in silence, only interrupted by a crying child downstairs, and the next-door neighbor practicing the flute, while the couple upstairs continued their nightly fight.

After a while, Max asked, "Have you ever thought of leaving?"

"Leaving?" She looked at him, incredulous, until she realized the enormity of his words. "You mean the GDR?" she asked in a whisper.

Max nodded. "Yes, the economy is so much better in the West. I see it every day when traveling through their sectors. Who doesn't want to improve their living conditions and opportunities?"

"But...but...that's illegal," she murmured, fear chilling her blood. "How can you even consider such a thing?"

"Sitting here and watching you afraid to have a normal discussion is enough to make me want a change."

"Things are far from perfect," she replied softly. "But that's hardly a reason to leave your country. In any case, it's just temporary; soon we'll all live in prosperity."

"Blessed are the poor in spirit," he teased her. "You really shouldn't believe everything you hear on the radio. Talking about radio, it was also illegal to listen the BBC."

"That was different, we were at war." She scrunched up her nose, considering his question. "I don't think I would ever want to leave. I don't know anyone in the West. Besides, there have been improvements in living conditions and wages, perhaps not as many as we'd like, but still..."

"Our system is morally superior." Max ran a hand through his hair. "I just wish our government would actually listen to its people."

"Now, that would make a nice change, wouldn't it?" Flori loved many things about her country, but the new government wasn't one of them, even though things were arguably a lot better than during the war.

CHAPTER 2

Moscow, 5th of March 1953

C olonel Vladimir Rublev arrived at the foremost citadel, the majestic seat of Russian power. The Kremlin's grandeur never failed to impress him, with its towering walls, intricate architecture, and centuries of history embedded within the imposing stone structure. As he walked through the massive gate, he briskly brushed off the snow that had settled on his thick gray coat.

A guard greeted him. Returning the gesture with a nod and a salute, Vladi couldn't help but comment on the lingering winter, his breath visibly misting up the cold air. "Winter is still refusing to leave Moscow."

Behind his breezy demeanor, however, lay an exhaustion that consumed him. It had been a long day filled with back-to-back meetings, focusing on intense discussions and strategic planning. As a high-ranking officer in the Red Army Intelligence, Vladi was accustomed to give his all at work. Now he craved an evening of revelry, hoping to drown his fatigue in a haze of intoxication and wake up the next morning in the arms of an alluring woman. It was the perfect recipe for an escape from the weight on his broad shoulders, a temporary reprieve from the responsibilities that governed his existence.

His boots clacked noisily on the marble floor as he walked through the corridors of power. The Kremlin's charged atmosphere was palpable. This was the place where ambitions clashed, alliances were forged and broken, as were promises, and dreams came true or died.

However, Vladi pushed aside thoughts of politics and power plays. When the secretary approached with a worried look on his face, Vladi knew his boss had plans for him that would not coincide with his own.

"Colonel Rublev, so good that you're here." The man's stiff shoulders drooped. "I have been trying to locate you all afternoon."

"Well, I'm here now." Vladi groaned, since there wouldn't be time for the pleasure he had planned this evening. "What is it that requires my presence? What can I do for you?"

"General Propov wants to see you, urgently."

Vladi suppressed another groan. He'd hoped to dodge giving his boss the day's summary until the following morning. Forcing a fake cheeriness he was far from feeling, he gave a curt nod and asked sarcastically, "By urgently, I suppose you mean right now?"

"I'm afraid so, though yesterday would have been preferable to the General," the secretary replied, returning the jibe with a bit of his own irony. "Go right in, he's waiting for you, comrade."

Squaring his shoulders, Vladi walked toward his boss's office. If General Propov required his presence, he'd better obey. He knocked on the solid, intricately carved wooden door and barely had time to take a breath before the General's booming voice called him in.

The uniformed man behind the grand desk presented an impressive stature, countless medals on his chest giving testimony to his heroic acts in the Great Patriotic War.

"Comrade Rublev, come in. Please have a seat." The General's shrewd eyes scanned Vladi, apparently noticing the tired lines in his face, because he added amiably, "Would you like a vodka?"

"Thank you comrade, I could really use a drink." Vladi wondered what he was in for. The tension in the room warned him something odd was going on. "I have spent the entire day with delegations from socialist brother countries, discussing the worrisome increase in criticism against Soviet directives. This hostile attitude must be stopped."

"It will be dealt with as soon as your report goes upstairs," Propov replied as he poured two glasses of vodka. "But that can wait. There's something else I want to discuss with you."

Vladi's heart sank. It must be very serious indeed to require two vodkas. What could it be? Nonetheless, he kept his mouth shut, having learned from experience that the general didn't appreciate questions. Vladi took the offered seat and waited patiently, observing his superior. He'd served under Propov for more than a decade and they knew each other well. They'd survived the Great Patriotic War together, had been deployed to Berlin for a couple of years, and had both returned to Moscow four years ago.

Right now, General Propov looked old and tired, but Vladi knew that looks were often deceptive. His boss had a sharp mind and the necessary shrewdness to remain in a position of power. Today, deep lines were etched on his face and a slight tremor shook his hands as he carried the two full glasses from the antique oak cabinet – no doubt one of the spoils of war from a rich German household – to the equally fine oak desk with the mammoth chair behind it.

The old man's perpetually red-glowing nose and the swollen bags beneath his eyes attested to a high alcohol consumption and an acute lack of sleep. Even as Vladi's curiosity grew about the reasons for the old man's attitude, Propov handed one glass to him and settled back into his chair.

Vladi nervously sipped his. There was still no word of explanation for this meeting. Propov downed his own drink in one gulp and fixed his cold blue eyes on Vladi. Sweat trickled down Vladi's back as he feverishly racked his brain to recall any misdemeanor he might have committed.

"Comrade Stalin is dead." Propov delivered this stunning news

14

calmly, as if he had revealed that the weather would be cold with a chance of rain.

Vladi's hands began to shake, forcing him to grip the glass more firmly. His stomach clenched with nausea. He'd never imagined this might be what Propov would announce, and the news had hit him like a bolt out of the blue.

Fearing that he might be physically sick, but aware that his reaction was being closely observed, Vladi managed to quickly compose himself.

He tried to find an appropriate response, but his throat dried up as his mind reeled. What should he say about the death of a man who had, for over a quarter of a century, held the Soviet Union and half of Europe in his unyielding grasp, establishing himself as a godlike figure, an all-knowing leader. Loved by some and feared by many, Stalin had ruthlessly governed with an iron fist, indiscriminately eliminating both foes and friends, leaving a trail of destruction in his wake.

Vladi had grown up under the shadow of Stalin's regime, witnessing the pervasive reach of his control. Dissent was swiftly crushed and the consequences for speaking out against the regime were severe: imprisonment, exile, or worse. During his formative years in the Komsomol, Vladi had learned to tread carefully, to never voice a single word of criticism against the great leader, however well-intentioned it might be.

Propov's announcement of Stalin's death was utterly unexpected. After all, gods were supposed to be immortal. The omniscient Soviet leader had been a looming presence throughout Vladi's life, but now with Stalin gone he wondered what the future might hold.

"Comrade Stalin was at his Kuntsevo Dacha when he suffered a stroke." Propov broke the silence. "He was only seventy-four years old, much too young to die."

Vladi shivered involuntarily, unable to reply. Instead, he nodded his head in agreement. He held onto his glass, downing the entire content in one gulp, relishing the sharp burn on its way down his throat, lighting a fire in his stomach.

In that moment he realized Stalin's death was going to change everything. If for the better or worse would depend entirely on Vladi's actions throughout the following weeks.

"This is horrible news," he finally managed to croak.

A long silence ensued, during which General Propov studied Vladi closely, making him feel as if he were a lab rat about to be dissected. It cost him all his willpower to remain absolutely still and not show the slightest trace of anxiety.

Finally, Propov leaned back in his chair. His eyes didn't betray any emotion. "Indeed, it is the worst news. Not only for the country as a whole but for us in particular."

Vladi gave a nod, surprised by the sharing of a candid opinion. Mentioning one's own prospects, tied in with the death of a national hero, verged on blasphemy. People were exiled or shot for less. It was such a bold statement that Vladi clasped his hands together to keep them from trembling. He sensed General Propov's observant eyes on him and realized any sign of weakness or disloyalty might lead to his downfall. His only hope was that the potent alcohol would trade his fear for courage.

"As always, you're correct in your assessment." Vladi always wholeheartedly agreed with his superiors, because stating his true opinion might prove fatal.

"Will you get the bottle, please? We're going to need it." The general lit a cigar and slowly inhaled.

"Of course, Comrade General." Vladi walked over to the beautiful cabinet and picked up the vodka. "Shall I pour?"

"Please. Help yourself, and make mine a stiff one."

Vladi's pulse raced, making him struggle to remain outwardly calm. His hands continued to tremble a little as he returned to his chair to pour the drinks and place the half empty bottle on the desk.

"To us!" General Propov toasted.

"To us." Confused by the peculiar situation, Vladi took a gulp, again savoring the fiery burn of the vodka. The next minutes might decide about his future, but he knew better than to ask outright.

Instead, he waited for Propov to speak again, hoping his boss would reveal a hint of what was to come.

"Lavrentiy Beria told me a few days ago that Comrade Stalin had suffered from a stroke and might well be fighting his last battle." General Propov began to speak in slow, well considered words. Beria was head of the secret service and thus Vladi's supreme chief. He was also among Stalin's four closest confidantes, the others being Nikita Khrushchev, the First Secretary of the Communist Party; Georgy Malenkov, Stalin's deputy; and Nikolai Bulganin, member of the almighty Politburo. Inevitably, one of them would become the new leader of the Soviet Union.

"Unfortunately, the great Stalin never regained full consciousness or the faculty of speech." Propov poured himself another glass of vodka.

"That is very lamentable." These words of sympathy would be expected.

Just a few months ago, Stalin had ousted his long-time companions - Vyacheslav Molotov and Anastas Mikoyan - so the fight for the first office in the state was going to be fought just between the "big four", as Vladi secretly called them. Since nobody could predict which one of them would prevail, it was both an opportunity and a threat at the same time.

One should not too openly support one candidate, for fear of annoying another one. To make matters even more complicated, Beria was not only Vladi's and Propov's supreme chief, but also a good friend and mentor to the general.

"The public will be informed about our beloved leader's death tomorrow morning, which gives us all night to prepare." Propov's tone was conspiratorial.

"I am at your disposal." Stalin's death had changed everything, not only in the grand scheme of things, but had also put the kibosh on Vladi's personal plan to conclude the exhausting day in a bar, and later spending the night in the arms of a willing woman.

"We must get to work right away," Propov said, generously

pouring another vodka for both of them. "Over the next few days you'll report exclusively to me, working on my orders alone."

"Understood."

"We need to secure the support of key military and party officials." Propov presented his plan. "You can use any tactics you see fit, ranging from discussions to bribes or threats. Just make sure you bring them into Beria's camp."

Vladi nodded. Propov had patently prepared in advance for this situation. A rush of excitement raced through his body, since this was a task much to his liking. He had to tread carefully with higher-ups, but had no qualms about lesser mortals. Harassing lower ranks, issuing threats, even using a bit of physical persuasion on recalcitrant subjects, when necessary, immediately came to his mind.

"Within the hour, everyone of importance will arrive at the Kremlin. Go out and mingle with every last one of them. Talk to their secretaries and aides - those chaps know everything. Report back to me in the morning. I want to know exactly what's going on."

"Yes, comrade." Vladi stood to attention. "I'm honored to be under your command during this important time."

"We've had our differences in the past." General Propov raised a hand. "Nevertheless, I must admit you get the required results."

Vladi found it difficult to keep a grin spreading from ear to ear. His boss was usually extremely sparing with praise, so a compliment for his right-hand man was a big deal indeed.

"Thank you, comrade."

"Just another thing I must mention." Propov motioned for Vladi to sit down again. "The next days, possibly weeks, will be turbulent. The inner circle will be in disarray. I know for a fact that Malenkov and Bulganin are already jockeying for position, trying to gain the upper hand in the power struggle. Also, we can't rule out Molotov and Mikojan yet, as they might grab the opportunity to return to power. Whilst our first loyalty is to Beria, we do need to stay on the good side of the other ones as well. We can't afford to miss a single opportunity."

"Whatever you wish, comrade."

A wry smile flitted across Propov's thin lips. "I know of your penchant for doing things in a non-conventional way. I don't usually appreciate it, though I believe your methods will work in our favor in the current circumstances. Just do me one favor: put on your damn uniform."

"I'll do so right away, comrade." Vladi always kept a spare uniform in his office, since the wearing of it or not was a constant point of friction between him and his boss. As part of the Red Army Intelligence, Vladi rather worked in obscurity, preferring to wear his own kind of uniform: a pair of sturdy black pants, a shirt with the top two buttons left open and a black leather jacket, just like his idol, the heavyweight boxing champion of the USSR, Nikolay Korolyov.

This had been Vladi's mode of operation for the past decade and it had served him well, both with his professional tasks and with the ladies, who invariably fell for his bad-boy charm. Admittedly, the shoulder epaulettes of a colonel also excited many women, especially a certain type. He wasn't selective where women were concerned: as long as she was willing to have sex, with no strings attached, he never declined a genuine offer.

"Off you go. There's a lot of work to do," Propov ordered, probably ready for some shut-eye after the events of the past days.

Leaving the room, Vladi recognized his future was far from secure. Granted, the death of Stalin may have opened up new possibilities, but it had also created new dangers.

CHAPTER 3

Katja and her classmate Liese climbed the six-foot stone wall separating the school grounds from the main road. They sat dangling their legs and soaking up the warm rays of sunshine, a welcome change after a brutally cold winter. Summer was around the corner and nothing was going to dampen their spirits on this beautiful day.

"Can you believe it, Liese? I can't believe we're graduating in just a few months." Katja raised her arms in the air, her hands reaching up to the sky. "Freedom! We'll finally be free." Yet Katja was hardly a slave; her sister Flori made sure she had what she needed.

"You're funny. There's no freedom in this country." Liese scoffed at the idea as she put one foot on the wall. She teetered dangerously for a moment and made Katja gasp.

"Watch out!" In fear of her classmate toppling backwards to the ground – outside the school yard no less – Katja quickly grabbed Liese's arm. "Don't do that, it makes my stomach queasy just looking at you."

"Look at me, I'm flying!" Liese laughed off the concern as she leaned backward, stretching out her arms and legs and waving them about.

"Please stop!" Katja begged.

Liese, though, was undeterred and continued to show off her acrobatic skills, her eyes twinkling with mischief. "Want to see what I can do?"

"No, I do not. I'm getting down. And you should come with me."

"How about this?" In one swift movement, the slim, flexible girl raised herself to a standing position, then stretched out her legs and arms like a gymnast on a balancing beam.

"Oh, my God! What do you think you're doing? For God's sake, get down and let's get back to class," Katja cried, as she jumped down herself and waited for Liese to join her. When she turned, she saw her friend was still on the wall, an annoyed look on her face.

"Get down for God's sake, will you! You'll lose balance and break your neck." Katja's head dizzied with vertigo just by looking at her. "Come on, Liese, please, I don't want to get into trouble!"

"Never take God's name in vain. I hate it when you do that, I've told you so before." Liese glared at her, brows furrowed, as if she'd swoop from her perch to personally punish such a grave sin.

"Calm down, for heaven's sake." Katja laughed. "God's not going to strike me dead for mentioning Him, is He?"

"It's not a joke, so please stop." Liese pouted, jumping into the air and gracefully landing again on the narrow wall.

"You're going to give me a heart attack if you don't get down from there immediately." Shivers raced down Katja's spine as she imagined all the horrible accidents that might happen if Liese continued doing silly acrobatics up there just to prove a point.

"If you insist, your highness." Liese curtsied, much too deep, and then made a cartwheel from the wall. She bowed like a gymnast and threw her arms out as she stood firm on the ground.

Katja's jaw dropped to the floor, her heart missing a beat or two. "That was awesome. You should have become a gymnast."

"I won the GDR championship in my age group three years ago." Despite the stellar achievement, Liese's voice was sullen.

"Really? Why did you never tell me?"

"It wasn't such a big deal." Liese shrugged and walked toward the school building.

"Nonsense. That's huge. As in really huge. There are only – how many? A few thousand? – gymnasts competing for that title." If Katja had achieved something so prestigious she'd be shouting it from the rooftops. Liese though, never spoke much. She and her mother had moved to Treptow at the beginning of the school year. Leaning back and scrutinizing her, Katja realized that she didn't know all that much about the other girl, except that she was a devout Christian. "Why didn't you continue?"

Liese looked around the school yard, inhaling deeply as she gazed at the linden trees proudly displaying their first green leaves of the year. Despite nobody else being within hearing range, she lowered her voice to a whisper. "They kicked me out of the national squad because I'm a Christian."

"Oh, I'm so sorry." Katja didn't know what else to say. Of course she knew about the official policy to separate state and church, but she'd never once considered that being a Christian would have such severe repercussions.

Liese waved her hand, trying to appear dismissive. "Don't worry, I've grown too old anyway. My mother always says it might have been for my own good, since she hated the dangerous moves we practiced. Just like you, she couldn't bear watching me doing a back handspring on the balance beam."

Katja swallowed hard. Her own talents definitely lay in the field of natural sciences, not sports. It was hard to get her head around someone being sidelined for their beliefs, so she changed the topic. "What do you want to do after school?"

"Me?" Liese's face became dreamy. "I'd love to be a teacher; an elementary school teacher, to be precise."

"Really?" Katja couldn't imagine anyone enjoying to spend their time with loud, snotty, demanding children. "Have you applied?"

"I did." Liese huffed out a deep breath. "They put me on a waiting list...for being a Christian, so there goes that dream up in smoke!"

"The ruling SED has done its best to suppress the influence of religion." Katja helplessly repeated what their politics teacher had told them.

They walked toward the entrance to the school building with four minutes left before the next class would start. Katja glanced at the other girl out of the corner of her eye, taking in the finely chiseled features, the pale skin with thousands of freckles, the ash-blonde hair tied into a ponytail, and the mouth that never seemed to laugh. A wave of sympathy hit her and she put her hand on Liese's arm. "If it gives you so much grief, why don't you pretend you're not a Christian?"

Liese stopped dead in her tracks, her face a mask of horror mixed with disgust. "I cannot do that. The Bible tells us how Petrus denied Jesus three times, before he found his courage when the cock crowed." She put a hand over her heart. "I must be brave and do what is right, in spite of the consequences. I shall never deny my savior."

"Surely your God would understand and forgive you if you acted for the sake of your future?" Katja asked curiously. "If you can better yourself you can do more for your family and your community. Surely that means something?"

"Please don't speak so frivolously about God. Faith isn't something you can put on and take off like a set of clothes. It's who I am, God is a part of me." Liese was unreasonably upset.

"Feels odd to me that we can't have a normal discussion about something you feel so strongly about," Katja said huffily. "It's just like not being allowed to ask questions about the people who are running our country or why certain promises that were made by these leaders are not being met...or why the authorities are not allowing people to live according to their religious beliefs."

Liese remained stone faced and walked to her seat without responding.

Katja found her friend's behavior foolish rather than brave. She had no qualms herself about pretending to follow the SED party line to attain her goals. She certainly wouldn't sacrifice her aspirations, to enroll at the prestigious Humboldt University, for a man who'd died almost two thousand years ago.

Shrugging, she decided Liese's religious conviction wasn't her problem. She had more pressing issues to deal with. Her Russian language skills, for example. Every student had to prove a mastery of Russian to enter university, and while Katja was a math wizard, she struggled with the non-scientific subjects.

But she was determined to do whatever it took to stand on her own feet and escape the sometimes oppressive protectiveness of her sister. She loved Flori to bits, grateful that her older sister had raised her and made sure she could pursue her dreams, but she still yearned to live her own life. Going to university was the best way to do so.

Meanwhile, they had reached the hallway filled with students milling about and Katja couldn't press the issue for fear of someone overhearing them and reporting any perceived or actual criticism of the regime to the school administration. She wouldn't be the first student to get into trouble for subversive talk. As they slipped into the classroom, Katja gazed over to her friend, regretting their row.

"Want to meet later this week to go over the geography homework?" she asked, hoping to mend the rift. On that occasion she would ask Liese more questions about her past as a gymnast, which seemed a rather glamorous sport.

"I'd love to." Liese smiled, her pique already forgotten. "The lesson on the achievements of the Soviet Union, in using forces of nature to generate energy, was so confusing."

"Old Herr Fischer often teaches contradictory things. In one sentence he claims that private property is the root of all evil, in the next he prattles on about the decline in production after nationalization, chalking it up to farmers clinging to outdated societal models." Inwardly, Katja shrugged, preferring to stick to things that could be mathematically proven. That way, at least, there were no opinions, or dreams. Things either were true or false, independent of circumstances, time or other variables.

CHAPTER 4

F lori arrived at the entrance gate of the chocolate factory shortly before six o'clock, just in time for the early shift.

"Good morning, Fräulein Eilers," the stocky, gray-haired guard greeted her while he opened the gate.

"Good morning, Herr Wacker. How is your wife?" Flori liked the old man who always had a smile for her, regardless of weather or time of day. His wife had recently suffered from a serious bout of rheumatism, which had required hospitalization.

Julia Wacker was well known by the workers since her husband never failed to mention her. After thirty years of marriage the two were still so much in love it was always "Frau Wacker said this," or "Julia thinks that."

"Much better, thanks to the good doctors at the Charité." He grinned from ear to ear. "My Julia will be home by next week."

"Tell her I send my best wishes for a full recovery." Flori gave him a smile and walked through the gate into the factory premises. In the locker room, she changed into the drab gray uniform all employees had to wear. She checked herself in the mirror, satisfied that not a single strand of her golden blonde hair escaped the bun at the nape of her neck.

"Need help?" Carolin, one of her co-workers asked, rushing into the changing room at the last minute.

"No thanks," Flori mumbled between pressed lips, where she held two hair pins required to keep the mandatory hairnet in place. No worker was allowed on the floor with exposed loose hair for fear it might fall into the chocolate. "There, I'm done!"

"You look so glamorous, Flori, you can't hide it no matter how severely you dress yourself." Carolin laughed, tossing her own magnificent chestnut-colored hip-length hair over her shoulder.

Flori blushed, not sure whether Carolin was joking or not. To deflect the attention from herself, she offered, "Would you like me to quickly plait your hair?"

"I wish they'd let us wear it loose." Carolin sighed dramatically, despite a nodded agreement and positioning herself in front of Flori, who divided the lush hair into three parts, making a long braid, which she wrapped around her co-worker's head, fixing it in place with the hated hairnet and several pins.

"There you go, we wouldn't want it to get entangled in one of the machines, would we?"

"Thank you, although I'd love to dip it in the chocolate. My husband would go all crazy licking it clean. The hair...and more..." Carolin pursed her lips at the salacious remark.

"Please, no details." Flori put up her hands in defense, since Carolin had a penchant for divulging intimate details. In that moment, Klara dashed in, late as usual.

"Morning, ladies," she greeted breezily. "Cover up for me? I'll be there in a minute."

"Sure," the others replied, since this happened too often to count. Even salary deductions for not being on time didn't seem to make Klara more conscientious about her lack of punctuality. Her hair was cropped short in military style, which saved her valuable time in not having to fix hair pins to make it stay beneath the hairnet.

While Klara hung her coat in her locker and tucked her purse behind it, the others walked over to their workplace, chatting up the foreman so he wouldn't notice that Klara lagged behind.

"A few of us are planning a girls' night out soon. You should join us," Carolin suggested.

"Thank you, but..." Flori would love to go, yet she hesitated because she didn't want to leave Katja alone. It was irrational, since her little sister was about to graduate from high school in a few months and could well care for herself.

"Come on, Flori, it'll be fun! How are you ever going to meet Mr. Right if you bury yourself in work?"

Flori was relieved of an answer by Klara, who was rushing down the corridor to her work station, to arrive a split-second before Herr Schmidt, the foreman, stepped out of his office.

"Late again, Fräulein Klara." Schmidt wagged his fat finger at her, which meant he intended to dock her wages.

"Not too late. See?" She gave him her sweetest smile and pointed up to the huge clock hanging from the roof, where the minute hand sprung to the twelve in that very moment.

He gave her a scolding stare. Klara wasn't intimidated though, since she knew how to deal with him and got away with it, more often than not, by batting her eyelashes as she explained why she was late.

"Go now. Off to work." Schmidt waved his hands in a shooing motion, before he beckoned Flori to follow him to his desk at the end of the long grinding room, from where he kept an eagle eye on his crew.

Behind his back, Klara made a goofy face, causing Flori to shake her head at the incorrigible woman. Beside her, Carolin broke out into a fit of giggles, which she disguised as a cough.

Carolin also often used her femininity to her advantage, especially after work when she flipped her gorgeous hair behind her shoulders with a well-practiced movement most men salivated over.

"Mmm...what a delicious aroma! Must have been a new delivery of cocoa beans," Flori said, while wondering what the foreman might want from her. "Good morning, Herr Schmidt. You want to see me; what's up?"

"Our Dutch supplier has sent a new batch. The night shift has already roasted the cocoa beans. If you manage it carefully, there'll be enough to make a small amount of real chocolate for the national market as well."

Strangers always assumed that working in a chocolate factory meant the women indulged in sweet delicacies all day long, which couldn't be further from the truth. Apart from the fact that ninety percent of the time the factory resorted to producing Vitalade due to a shortage of cocoa beans, the work was back-breaking. And obviously the women never got to savor the treats they made – apart from inhaling the rich sweet smell or maybe tasting a few morsels they swept from the tables when cleaning up for the next shift.

"We ladies will do our best as always, Herr Schmidt."

"I know, I know. The reason why I asked you to come see me is that we have ten new workers in today. And I want you to teach the newcomers about their duties. Take them through the stages of the process from start to finish."

"Yes, Herr Schmidt," Flori dutifully answered. Whereas most of her colleagues loathed having to explain the tasks to new workers, she enjoyed it. It gave her time away from the grind to see the bigger picture and find joy in watching how the different raw materials underwent processing until a beautiful, aromatic delicacy came out as the end product.

It was almost like designing a dress: in the beginning there was cloth and thread, in the end a garment that enhanced a woman's beauty, making her irresistible. Flori aspired to fill her country with prettiness.

The newcomers stared at her with wide-open eyes, listening intently to the explanations as they followed her from process to process. "Before the beans arrive here, they are harvested from pods, fermented for several days in wooden boxes and then sun-dried, cracked and winnowed to separate the nibs from the shells. Only the nibs are used to make chocolate." Flori pointed at the bags of beans piled high in the warehouse.

"Our task in the factory," Flori continued, while she walked the new employees through each step of the chocolate-making process.

"The beans are roasted in those large ovens over there, during which they have to be monitored constantly. Exact temperatures must be maintained, hot enough to evaporate moisture and acid inside the beans, as well as kill bacteria, but cool enough not to damage the precious flavor of the nib."

"I never thought it would be this complicated," one of the girls remarked.

"You'll learn quickly." Flori remembered her own anxiety when she'd first started to work here. Everything had been so new, seemed so complicated. Now it was second nature to her. "Just keep an eye on what you're doing and never leave your station unattended. Due to the Western Imperialists making imports difficult, cocoa is a scarce raw material."

A redhead with the most beautiful green eyes, cocked her head, murmuring, "And here's me thinking it was because we lack hard currency."

Involuntarily, Flori ducked her head. The redhead's statement could be seen as criticizing the government which was, if not exactly forbidden, highly discouraged. Everyone knew the young nation had teething problems and needed time to overcome them. Flogging the minor shortcomings to death served no one. As the person tasked to train the new arrivals, Flori was supposed to report such behavior to the foreman, yet she couldn't bring herself to get the friendly-looking woman into trouble, so she pretended not to have heard.

"As I said, cocoa is expensive, therefore mistakes are costly and might result in stopping the entire production for weeks. The "roasting girls", as we call them, have to be very alert at all times. That's why we have a rotation system, so nobody will be roasting more than two hours at a time."

A look of fear passed round the group and Flori soothed them. "Most employees settle in without a problem so don't worry and do your best. During your first days you'll be assigned to the easier tasks."

A nervous laugh eased the tension and they moved onto the next stage.

"The nibs are ground into a thick paste called cocoa mass or chocolate liquor." She pointed out the "grinding girls" doing their job. "This paste is pressed to extract the cocoa butter and leave behind the cocoa cake. The cake is then pulverized into powder, which we sell for baking purposes or for hot chocolate. What remains is the cocoa butter. We mix it with sugar and other ingredients to make different types of chocolate, such as dark, milk or white. The mixture is refined and tempered to improve the texture and flavor. Finally, the chocolate is molded into bars or shapes and wrapped ready for sale."

"So, can we buy chocolate?" a blonde girl asked.

"Unfortunately not. The real chocolate is produced exclusively for our Dutch client, who also provides the cocoa for us." Flori's eyes sought the redhead's, sending her a warning gaze not to broach the topic of missing hard currency again. "Sometimes there's a small batch we can sell for the national market, but usually it's Vitalade for us."

After her shift, Flori hurried home, hoping Katja had not forgotten to pass by the butcher. Once a month, it was slaughtering day. Not that they were able to afford the best meat, but at least they could buy a few sausages to spice up the daily potato dish.

She arrived home to find Katja and a classmate sitting at the kitchen table, going over their homework.

"Hello girls, studying for the final exams?"

"Hello Flori, this is my friend Liese. You remember I told you that she moved here at the beginning of the school year?"

"Oh yes. Nice to meet you." Flori smiled at Liese, before she turned toward Katja. "Did you pass by the butcher?"

"Sure." Katja grinned. "His wife gave me some extra liverwurst to fatten me up."

Guilt sent heated flashes into Flori's face. The two of them had gone hungry for years before she'd found the factory work. Even now, Katja was much thinner than she should be.

"Would you like to stay for dinner?" she asked Liese.

"No, thank you. I have Bible study group tonight at the Junge Gemeinde."

Flori did her best not to let the shock show on her face and feigned a friendly smile. "I'll leave you girls to study then."

Escaping into the kitchen to prepare the liverwurst for dinner, Flori fought with her emotions. It wasn't that she disliked the Christians, per se, some of them were very fine people. The problem was that the government did not allow a youth organization other than the state-sanctioned FDJ, the Free German Youth. In the eyes of the communists, religion, and thus the Junge Gemeinde as a religious organization, exploited the oppressed masses by promising a better life in the hereafter, thereby diverting them from participating in any national class struggles.

Just a few months prior, she'd listened to a lengthy discussion on the radio about the dangers of the Junge Gemeinde. To mitigate the threat, the Politburo had been forced to adopt a plan for exposing the Junge Gemeinde as a front organization for warmongering, sabotage and espionage directed by West German and American imperialist forces. Katja might get into severe trouble for mixing with members of an anti-state organization.

When Liese finally left, Flori darted into the living room. "Did you know that Liese is a member of Junge Gemeinde?"

"So what? I like her. You know, she was a gymnast, even won the GDR championship in her age group."

"Good for her." Flori furrowed her brows, since she had been under the impression that members of religious groups were excluded from most activities, certainly from prestigious sports. "In any case, you shouldn't keep her company, it will only fall back on you."

Katja waved her concerns away. "You're always fear-mongering. She's a classmate, not my lover."

"Dear God! Being a lesbian is not a joke. That can get you in worse trouble than being a Christian."

"Calm down. I'm very much into men." Katja licked her lips in a very inappropriate manner, making Flori aware of just how much her little sister had grown up. "By the way, I have already advised Liese to pretend to be an atheist, for an easier life."

"And?" Flori would never have guessed that Katja could be so sensible.

"She refused."

At times, Flori hated her sister for being so brief. Everything had to be wormed out of her. "Did she say why? It's not exactly a smart move."

"That's what I told her and she got all preachy on me, prattling on about moral integrity and not betraying Jesus." Katja shrugged. "It's her life, not mine."

"You might want to steer clear of her," Flori said, relieved at her sister's prudent attitude. It wasn't that she bought into all that communist stuff. After all, she'd joined the SED for the sole reason that party members received promotions and others didn't. And God knew how dearly they needed the money.

While education itself was free, she still needed to buy school stationery for Katja, who'd become a straight-A student after some adjustment problems to the political pressure in the newly-founded GDR.

Pride warmed Flori's heart. Her little sister was on track to be assigned a place at the prestigious Humboldt University for engineering after passing the screening tests with flying colors, due to her outstanding talent for mathematics, along with a bit of help from Max.

"Don't worry so much," Katja said as she cleared away her homework to set the table for dinner. "I'll be fine."

CHAPTER 5

After changing into his uniform, Vladi stepped into the hallway, where the tense atmosphere hit him like a dip in an icy lake. The usually serene and quiet Kremlin was filled with men of every rank and name, and apparently each with the same task Vladi had.

Forging alliances, pulling in favors and getting themselves into prime position with whoever could become the new Soviet leader was the aim. Stalin's death had created an internal power vacuum, which was going to trigger a fierce struggle for succession. Various factions would be vying for control. Already, some contenders positioned themselves for a period of political infighting and uncertainty.

Vladi observed the men hurrying up and down the Kremlin hallway, keen to catch newcomers before others got to them. Tall and broad-shouldered, his presence was instantly noticed and it didn't take long until he was surrounded by men, some more important than others.

He began his relentless mission by mingling with officials, gathering information and making connections with those who might be useful to him. With unwavering determination, he skillfully maneuvered through the labyrinth of power. He put on a show of friendly camaraderie with his fellow officers and political figures until he chanced upon his best friend, Grigori, who also worked for the intelligence department, albeit in a different unit.

"I hadn't expected this news," Grigori said, dispensing with the customary polite greeting.

"Nobody did." Adrenaline surged through Vladi's veins, heightening his senses. "Grand times ahead, eh, Grigori?"

"Grand or scary, take your pick."

"Either way, we'll get plenty of action. It's almost as exhilarating as when we were in the thick of combat during the battle of Berlin," Vladi reminisced, referring to his time in Berlin after Germany's capitulation.

"I was injured and almost captured. I can't believe we survived that bloody war," Grigori replied.

"Sure, it was cruel and demanding, yet I've never felt more alive than during combat."

"Are you suicidal or what? I rather enjoy my quiet life in Moscow."

Quiet wasn't all bad; in fact, Vladi's life was pretty darn good these days. For a while he'd enjoyed living the comfortable life of a colonel, showered with *pajoks*, the gifts from the party. He'd moved into a nice apartment in one of the best areas of Moscow, possessed the freedom to come and go to work whenever he liked, attended parties with the bigwigs, consumed an abundance of vodka...and women. He loved the perks of being a member of the secret service, but found the desk work utterly boring and itched to be back in the thick of it.

He wanted to do something useful instead of being confined to his desk. He yearned to be out in the field again. To experience the thrill, the heightened senses after a rush of adrenaline; this was what made life interesting.

"Quiet is good; action is better." He winked at Grigori. "How's Olga?"

Grigori broke into a huge grin that creased the lines around his eyes, raising his hand to show off a shiny new wedding band. "It's been pure bliss since we finally tied the knot. You should try it, you know."

"Not in this life. I rather enjoy a variety." Vladi groaned as he ran a hand through his cropped blond hair. He reveled unashamedly in womanizing, taking great pleasure in his pursuit of the opposite sex. A beautiful married woman was particularly attractive to him because she was discreet and understood about giving and receiving pleasure without needless sentiment or romantic expectations.

"Even you've got to grow up eventually." Grigori wasn't ready to stop trying to coax his friend into changing his mind. "One day, a woman will come along and you won't know how you ever existed without her."

"Luckily, that day is not today." Vladi laughed. "Let's focus on the task at hand and mingle."

For the rest of the night, Vladi tirelessly campaigned, participating in backroom meetings, listening to conspiracies and rumors of plots. He shared information, maintaining an illusion of giving. He memorized every single bit of information that might be useful in the weeks to come, while keeping anything of value close to his chest. After all, what distinguished him from the rest of the Kremlin lackeys were his years of experience as an underground investigator and interrogator.

Several days later, he was called to a meeting with General Propov and two important guests: Norbert Gentner and his wife Rosalie. Vladi knew them both well from his time in East Berlin. Norbert Gentner had been the head of a delegation of German émigrés in Moscow, sent to rebuild Berlin according to the Soviet model.

A member of the communist KPD party, Gentner had fled Nazi Germany in 1938 and arrived in Moscow three years later, where he'd met Stalin and had been trained to take over the government of a defeated Reich. Driven by his ambitions, Gentner had proved

Moscow's best representative in Germany, never shy to push a new, sometimes unpopular, directive onto the population.

An astute strategist, Gentner rapidly became the go-to man for economic or political affairs, a man with access to valuable networks, influential contacts, and insider knowledge, more powerful than even the GDR's prime minister Otto Grotewohl. General Propov often said, if one wanted things to be done promptly, then one better talk to Norbert first.

Rosalie wisely kept in the background, campaigning for her husband in her elegant, gentle way. She used to be a translator, an excellent Russian speaker with knowledge of both the language and the culture acquired from living many years in the Soviet Union during her youth.

Her many talents included beauty and poise, as well as a talent for organizing fabulous parties that were well-loved by the high-ranking officials in Berlin. How Vladi missed those good times.

"Despite the sad occasion, it's such a pleasure to see you again, Rosalie." He bestowed a kiss on her hand.

"You're such a charmer, Vladi." She was easily twenty years older than him, but his tactics worked on women of any age. "Norbert and I are both out of our minds with grief."

Vladi suspected they hadn't raced to Moscow the very moment they heard about Stalin's death out of respect for the old man alone. The Gentners had a lot to lose, so more likely they were here forging relationships in an effort to come out ahead, irrespective of who became the new Soviet leader.

"Comrade Norbert, my sincere condolences. The news of Comrade Stalin's death has been devastating for all of us."

"It has," General Propov chimed in, beckoning the guests to take seats at the round table in the corner of his office. "But now we must look ahead with a clear mind, and with the well-being of our great Soviet Union, and her dearest brother country the German Democratic Republic, always in our hearts."

"We're here to offer our support to you, Comrade General, and to whoever will follow in the steps of the greatest leader of all." Rosalie bestowed a heartfelt smile on Propov, her husband nodding in agreement.

On official business, where every nuance or unspoken word had importance, Norbert usually let his wife do the talking, since her mastery of the Russian language was so much better than his.

"I certainly am grateful for your continued support, as is Comrade Beria." Propov fixed his eyes on Norbert. "You may know that a successor has not been announced yet."

"We do." Norbert leaned forward.

Vladi secretly wondered who of the aspirants was Norbert's first choice. Beria was known for his iron fist, leading the NKVD and administering the Gulag system of labor camps. He was feared by many, loved by few. Norbert though, had profited from Beria's harsh reign over dissidents and might well favor him over the others.

"The demise of Stalin has triggered a profound wave of apprehension and uncertainty. It has gripped the hearts and minds of every single citizen in the Soviet Bloc," Propov said thoughtfully. "Your presence at the Kremlin is evidence of your concern for the well-being of your country and its people."

"It is our dearest wish to honor Stalin's memory, and to serve his successor in the same unconditional way we served him." Rosalie, well-versed in politics, always found the proper words. She opened her palms to demonstrate the honesty of her words.

"In turbulent times, such as these, it is a relief to have strong allies by our side." Propov droned on about the collective grief of the Soviet nation and, in fact, the world. Finally, he said, with a wave of his hand in Vladi's direction, "Let's have a drink."

Vladi got up and walked toward the cabinet, taking out a bottle of vodka.

"Not that one. The one in the glass cabinet. A special drink for a very special occasion," Propov said.

Dutifully, Vladi reached into the glass cabinet, where a fine bottle of vodka had been standing on display since Propov had moved into this office. Its value had gone up considerably due to the brand's recent win of a gold medal at the international trade show in Bern.

"A toast," Propov suggested after Vladi had poured four glasses and handed them out. He stood to attention, raising his glass high. The others followed suit. "To the greatest of leaders. May he rest in peace."

"To Stalin." Vladi and the Gentners played their parts like a well-rehearsed chorus.

"To a great future for the greatest of all nations," Propov continued.

"To the Soviet Union."

"May our next leader be as benevolent, visionary, and caring as Stalin was, the greatest friend of mankind." Propov emptied his glass, and glanced expectantly at his audience.

Calling Stalin a philanthropist might be a bit far-fetched, given that he'd murdered many millions of people, but who was Vladi to object? The man was dead, after all. In any case, now was not the time for critique. The current situation was treacherous, full of dangers lurking in the shadows.

Wholeheartedly supporting Propov was Vladi's best shot at coming out ahead, especially as it seemed Beria was the contender most likely to gain the position of head of state.

"To our next leader," Vladi yelled, the Gentners joining in.

Propov's face lit up with joy and he beckoned to Vladi to refill the glasses.

This time, Norbert proposed a toast. "To our great brother nation, the first among socialist nations."

"To the Soviet Union."

"Please let me elaborate on my husband's sentiments." Rosalie glanced at General Propov, as if asking for permission to speak. An unnecessary politeness, since she always acted as Norbert's translator and, furthermore, she and the general had known each other for many years.

"Go ahead, my dearest Rosalie." General Propov peered at her with such softness in his eyes that Vladi wondered whether the two of them were having an affair – and if her husband knew and sanctioned it for the sake of good relations with the Muscovite rulers.

"Despite our unspeakable grief over the death of our beloved leader..." Rosalie dabbed at her eyes, "...Norbert and I are happy to see you again, dearest Comrade General. Rest assured that whoever becomes the new leader of the Soviet Union will have the German Democratic Republic's unequivocal support."

After several more glasses of vodka, the group turned to analyzing the key figures in the power struggle for Stalin's succession: Malenkov, Molotov, Beria, and Khrushchev. Each one of them possessed a unique set of qualities.

"Georgy Malenkov was a close associate of Stalin's," Norbert said. "He's been a full member of the Politburo for years and he's the deputy Premier, second only to the great Stalin. It would be logical if he became the new leader."

Propov objected, "It might be the logical outcome, but Malenkov doesn't have the inner strength needed to become premier. Lavrentiy Beria, however, is not only a member of the Politburo and head of the NKVD, but also his influence reaches far beyond the Soviet Union and into our socialist brother countries, don't you agree?"

"Of course we agree. Beria possesses a network of spies and informants in every corner of Soviet society. We in the GDR rely heavily on his organization for many purposes, and we'd love to congratulate him in his new position as Soviet premier, but..." Rosalie brushed the general's shoulder with her fingers. "...many men in power consider him too ruthless for the office."

Vladi's jaw dropped to the floor, witnessing how Rosalie masterfully played Propov. If he had to assess her biggest strength, it would be the ability to butter up her counterpart while getting her own opposing view across. No wonder her husband had become the most powerful man in East Germany, despite not being the prime minister.

Perhaps Grigori was right with his advice to settle down. If Vladi found himself a woman like Rosalie, who'd become the biggest asset to her husband's career, he'd snap her up and marry her on the spot. Spurred by the devil, he decided to put Rosalie to the test.

"What about Vyacheslav Molotov, Rosalie?" Vladi asked. "He's known for his unwavering loyalty to Stalin, possesses a keen intellect and a sharp tongue. Furthermore, he's a seasoned diplomat, skilled in navigating international affairs and negotiating with foreign powers. Would he be your first choice?"

Rosalie was not intimidated in the least, a testament to her many years navigating the treacherous waters of high politics. "Ach, Vladi. You know I don't have favorites and neither does Norbert. We live to serve: our people, our nation and the great Soviet Union which has bestowed so much friendship on us after what the Nazis did to them." She smiled sweetly at him. "The GDR will stand behind whoever becomes the new Premier."

"I wholeheartedly agree with you. We are all in our positions because we want to serve." Vladi too, was a master at this game.

"We might be surprised by the underdog," Norbert said.

"You're not seriously suggesting that Nikita Khrushchev will become Premier?" Propov glared at Norbert, his face dangerously red. "Khrushchev is an outsider in the power struggle; he's nothing but the Secretary of the Moscow party organization."

Vladi didn't miss the warning gaze Rosalie sent her husband before she addressed Propov. "None of us seriously believes Khrushchev will come out the winner; the other contenders are so much better suited. Yet, it would be imprudent to rule him out altogether. He's risen through the ranks with charisma and boldness. A man of the people, capable of capturing the attention and support of the masses. That might be what is needed to calm the turbulent waters, even if he'll be hoisted into position only for representation, while the true power lies with someone else."

Propov took a deep breath and then broke out into laughter. "Good point. Just like Otto Grotewohl is your prime minister, but we all know in whose hands the true power lies."

"Which we owe to none other than Beria and his competent generals." Rosalie winked at Propov, insinuating that her husband personally owed his position to him.

Vladi couldn't believe how easily this woman twisted Propov around her little finger. He'd admired her before; her performance today was out of this world. It was regrettable that his time in Berlin had come to an end, because he could learn so much from her.

Two more vodka bottles were emptied that night until the four people staggered home, assuring each other of their unconditional support.

CHAPTER 6

"Have you heard?" Frank shouted, as he ran toward Katja the moment she entered the school building in the morning.

"Heard what?" She raised an eyebrow at Frank's agitation. He was usually a down-to-earth lad, almost bordering on phlegmatic.

"They're going to expel Liese and Dirk."

"Oh." Katja stopped dead in her tracks. As far as she knew, Liese had done nothing wrong. Or...had the teacher suspected she'd been cheating in her geography exam? However, that wouldn't explain why Dirk had also been expelled. "What have they done?"

Frank rolled his eyes at her. "How come you don't know? I thought you and Liese are friends?"

"We are. Kind of. Still, I have no idea what she did." Katja couldn't help but feel a mix of sympathy and dismay for Liese.

"You know she belongs to the Junge Gemeinde, right?"

Katja nodded, an uneasy feeling pooling in her gut as she feared where this was going.

"So she had the invitation to a youth meeting in her pocket, which she accidentally took out together with her math booklet after school. Our director saw it and she got a reprimand for illegal religious activities."

"That stupid girl. I told her not to flaunt her Christianity at school."

Now it was Frank's turn to raise an eyebrow. "She should never have gotten involved with that subversive group. Everyone knows they work on behalf of West Berlin's terror and espionage organizations, under the mask of religion, trying to split the unity of our youth."

"Who told you such a silly thing?" The government might not like the Christian communities, but they certainly had never done anything to undermine a peaceful collaboration.

"Haven't you read the recent article in the *Junge Welt*?"

"Heaven forbid." Katja read the drivel of the Free German Youth Organization, which was anything but free, exclusively when it was required for homework assignments. She didn't take the left-wing, extreme Marxist point of view any more seriously than the Nazis' fascist articles they studied in politics class. She seemed to be the only one who noticed that both parties used the same tactics to promote their agendas.

"You really should. Every member of the Free German Youth is required to have a broad understanding of current political events." Frank used his hands to stress the importance of his words.

"I would if I had the time." Katja smiled at Frank, a member of the student board, and apparently now a stalwart of the Free German Youth organization, which everyone wanting a higher education had to join, whether they wanted to or not.

Katja herself had done so on the day she turned fourteen, for the sole reason of increasing her chances to gain one of the coveted places at the Humboldt University. "So, Liese got a reprimand for having a religious leaflet in her backpack?"

"It gets worse. When asked whether she agreed that churches are the enemies of the state, she reacted all haughty and cited article 39 of our constitution, saying that every citizen of the German Democratic Republic has the right to profess a religious faith and to practice religious acts."

"What's wrong about knowing and living by our constitution?"

Katja barely managed to keep a sarcastic undertone from her voice. "Isn't that what we are taught in political science?"

Frank cast her a wry grin. "Not if said religious group is, in fact, a terrorist organization, working to destroy our republic for the interests of the imperial West."

"Right, I forgot that part." Katja let out a sigh. She was sick and tired of the mental gymnastics needed to justify the constant oppression in her country. She had been only nine years old when the Russians had saved Germany from the fascist Nazis, but that didn't keep her from seeing the similarities.

"You shouldn't take this so lightly. The Junge Gemeinde is a serious threat to peace and prosperity in our republic. Anyway, the whole thing escalated because Liese stubbornly insisted that the constitution guaranteed her the freedom of religion. Dirk chimed in to help her – and, you won't believe this— they found an invitation to this church meeting in his bag as well."

"How heinous." Katja had heard enough and itched to get away from Frank. Her time was too precious to be wasted on stupid politics.

"Darn right!" Frank seemed to grow a few centimeters as his posture straightened with pride and self-righteousness. He then announced, in an arrogant tone, "So, the school administration has organized a conference this afternoon with obligatory attendance for every student."

Katja suppressed a groan. She really had better things to do than spend a boring afternoon in the auditorium being bombarded with vicious propaganda. Unfortunately, there was no way she could get out of it.

During each class, Katja stared at the door, willing it to open to see her friend walk through with a smile on her face as if nothing had happened. She balled her hand into a fist, cursing Liese's stubbornness. If only she had pretended not to believe in God...or at least hadn't carried that stupid leaflet in her backpack. It wasn't until lunch break that Katja managed to sneak away and find her friend in the auditorium.

"Where have you been all morning?"

"I was called to the director's office." A visibly exhausted Liese put down her backpack and opened it to fetch her lunch package.

"Want to go sit on the wall while you tell me everything?"

"Good idea. Who'll be first?" Liese raced off the second she finished speaking, her long and slim legs hammering the ground in an effort to win the race.

Katja rolled her eyes at these antics. They weren't twelve anymore. When she arrived at the wall, Liese was already up there in a handstand. Her stomach clenched at the precarious sight and she covered her eyes with one hand. "Would you please stop doing that? It makes me nauseous."

A giggle filled the air. Seconds later a soft thud indicated that Liese had put her feet on the wall. "There you go. You can look again."

"Thank you." Katja took her friend's outstretched hand to climb the wall and sat on the edge, her feet dangling. "So, what did the director say?"

"If it had only been the director." Liese grimaced . "He'd called to his aid four more teachers and three party-loyal members of the student board. Together they descended on me like fire-spewing dragons, ready to roast me for their evening meal."

"You're exaggerating." Katja couldn't help but laugh at the image forming in her head.

"Not at all. They harped on about the terrorist agenda of the Junge Gemeinde and urged me to denounce my religion, thus returning to the bosom of the community. They even casually suggested I join the Free German Youth instead."

"I told you weeks ago to do that."

Liese glared at her with unconcealed fury. "You condone them trampling on my religious freedom?"

"No, I don't. I'm just trying to be pragmatic here. You can still believe in your God, just don't flaunt it."

"And I thought you were my friend." Liese pushed the last bite of her sandwich into her mouth, jumped off the wall and rushed away.

"Hey, Liese, wait…" Despite her shouts, Liese refused to look back, leaving Katja with a sickening feeling of guilt.

"It isn't wrong to avoid trouble," Katja murmured to herself as she climbed from the wall. Pressing her lips into a thin line she mused about the best way to navigate the party line while not giving up one's convictions.

If the constitution granted every citizen the right to practice a religion, was Liese correct in defending her right? Was Katja wrong in telling her to give in for the sake of convenience? Their politics teacher always impressed on them that the constitution stood above everything, so why didn't he take Liese's side?

Because they claim the Junge Gemeinde is a terrorist organization, a voice whispered in her head. She pouted in response. There was no proof whatsoever for that claim; except these days, the Stasi - the state secret service - didn't need proof. A denunciation was enough to send someone to jail, never to be seen again. Oh, how she hated the bigotry of the ruling party.

In the auditorium she joined her classmates in the first two rows on the right. Since one of their own was to be condemned, the prime seats were reserved for them. On the podium sat the director, flanked by two teachers and two men in gray suits, presumably Stasi agents. Katja shivered involuntarily, her mind jumping to the public execution she'd been forced to witness as a child during the Nazi reign.

"I hope this doesn't shine a bad light on us," whispered Margie, another of Katja's classmates.

"Never liked that girl. She always had a threatening air about her," Thorsten said.

Katja bit on her lip to prevent herself from bursting into laughter. Liese was by far the sweetest, most inoffensive girl in their class, whereas Thorsten was a muscular, athletic guy.

Glancing left and right, she gazed into tense faces, thin lips and disapproving gestures. The verdict had already been decided, and Liese was guilty. Hot-red fury snaked up Katja's spine, making her sit straighter. Minutes later, she perked up her ears as the director launched into a tirade condemning Liese and Dirk's betrayal of the community. In a country where the constitution, written only several years prior, guaranteed the freedom of speech, nobody was allowed to actually voice a differing opinion.

Liese sat in a corner, a policeman next to her. She wasn't allowed on the stage, perhaps they feared she might repeat how wrong all of this was. Katja angrily shook her head. Liese had only herself to blame for this mess. Like everyone else in the auditorium she knew exactly how this ostensibly democratic nation worked.

Why hadn't she listened to well-meant advice? Why did she have to defend the Junge Gemeinde? Katja herself had long ago decided that she wasn't going to destroy her chance of studying engineering for political opinions.

If school required her to mourn the late Stalin, whom she had despised, she would shed tears of devastation. If the government asked her to stop going to church meetings, she'd turn around and dedicate her time to physics homework instead. It was utterly stupid on Liese's part not to accept the realities in this country, persistently believing the rights, stipulated in the constitution, genuinely existed.

Later, after hours of tiring sermons by different speakers, the director raised his voice to announce, "Guilt has been proven. Now the punishment must be decided. True to the democratic spirit of our nation, we will vote to determine whether the two culprits, associated with terrorist religious groups, should be expelled from school."

"Of course they have to be expelled," Margie whispered. "I surely don't want to sit next to a traitor in class."

Katja sent her a scathing glance. "How can you say that? We all know this is a sham. Liese has done nothing wrong." Surprised by her own outburst, she returned her focus to the podium. Her conscience, though, nagged her to do something instead of just standing by while her friend's future was at stake.

But she froze in her seat, trying to convince herself that warning Liese had been enough and now the girl must bear the consequences of her actions.

"Who wants the two traitors expelled?" the director asked. Hands went up everywhere in the auditorium. A smug expression crept onto his face. "Any votes against?"

Without taking a conscious decision, Katja's hand went up. Shocked silence filled the room. All eyes landed on her. She quickly dropped her hand, turning to see if anyone else had joined her protest. Nobody had.

"I gather it was a mistake, since you took your hand down," the director said. Not waiting for her answer he continued, "The motion to expel the traitors is unanimously accepted."

"No!" Katja shot up, staring at the man who'd just dismissed her opposing vote. Torn between her normal behavior to conform to the oppressive system, and staying true to her sense of justice, she expressed in a much calmer voice, "I do not support the motion."

The reverberations of her dissent swept through the room like the shockwave of a bomb. Murmurs of scandal broke out at her challenge of the authority's grip on expectations; side glances were cast at her, showing every emotion from disdain, to respect and hope. Katja couldn't believe that her small defiance had caused such a profound impact.

The director quickly regained his aplomb. "Nonetheless, the motion has been accepted. The audience is dismissed."

Katja fell back into her chair, half waiting for the Stasi men to haul her away. Nothing happened. After all the students had left the auditorium, not one of her friends had offered a word of support. She was left to wonder whether one small act of resistance had ruined her entire future career.

When she finally approached the door, Frank was waiting for her. "That was an incredibly stupid thing to do."

"I know, I didn't mean to, it just happened." Her shoulders sagged, expressing the misery she felt within.

"They're giving you the opportunity to repent." Frank smiled kindly. "You should accept it, otherwise this incident is going to have repercussions."

"You mean they're going to punish me for voicing my opinion?"

"A dissenting opinion," Frank corrected her, before he nodded.

"They definitely are. The teachers' board hasn't reached an agreement yet. Someone has floated the idea that you're too politically unreliable to attend university. That's when I suggested a session of criticism and self-criticism."

Cold shivers ran down Katja's spine, though she wasn't sure what she feared more - ruining her career by not being allowed to study, or the brutal instrument of self-criticism, in which honesty and truth didn't matter, only a confession of imagined crimes and complete submission to the prevailing party line.

Faced with the very strong possibility of ending up as a factory worker like her sister, Katja swallowed down her pride. If the school board wanted her to apologize for speaking out, she was willing to grovel. "Please tell the board members that I am sorry. I shouldn't have voiced my opinion."

"I'm glad you accept your error." Frank seemed genuinely pleased. "It would have been such a shame if they expelled you as well."

"Thank you." Katja did her best to hide the shock reverberating through her bones. Expecting this to be the end of the unpleasant issue, she recoiled at Frank's next words.

"You'll receive an official invitation to your criticism and self-criticism session."

CHAPTER 7

May 1953

Following Stalin's death, the contenders had agreed to form a troika for the interim, nominating Malenkov as premier, with Molotov and Beria announced as first deputies.

Despite his obvious hunger for power, Beria seemed content with the situation. A fact, which Vladi hadn't quite understood until General Propov had explained to him the reasoning behind it. Malenkov was a close ally of Beria, the two of them going back decades. Being the second man behind a weak leader was often the best strategy in which to weather turbulent times.

General Propov expected a shift in the power structure within the next six months, when his mentor Beria would usurp the ultimate power, disarm his opponents, possibly sparing Malenkov, who'd helped him achieve his ambition.

When Vladi received an urgent summons from Propov, he fully expected to receive news about the change in leadership.

General Propov opened the meeting with, "We have a problem."

Vladi remained silent, awaiting further explanation.

"The entire situation is somewhat delicate, so it goes without saying that every word has to stay within these walls."

"Of course, Comrade General." Vladi's mind raced with questions. To warrant such secrecy, something very unusual must have happened.

"The GDR has requested our help with the population's rising discontent over our occupation troops, and with their own government. Some of the unions have threatened strikes."

"They should know a strike is only damaging themselves." Vladi repeated the talking points he'd been exposed to during his years of education at the Komsomol. In theory, workers had a right to go on strike, but in the Soviet Union nobody ever did, because that would damage the industrial progress, which in turn would hurt the very people who went on strike.

"Tell that to those louts!" Propov's voice boomed. "We have enough problems of our own, we don't need Germany to destabilize the entire region."

"I agree." Vladi feared that he'd be somehow made responsible for the East German problem and racked his brain for a way to shift the blame onto someone else.

"It seems everyone was waiting for Stalin to die, so they could then launch whatever folly their hearts desired. Misguided weasels!" Propov talked himself into a frenzy, the medals on his chest clinking with every word he hurled at Vladi. "Comrade Beria summoned me."

Now that *was* bad news. Vladi swallowed hard, feeling the blood drain from his face.

"We need to put an end to this. Our boss can't be campaigning for the ultimate power and at the same time be putting out fires all over Eastern Europe. So, he needs someone to do this for him." Propov's face showed a hint of pride, emboldening Vladi to speak up.

"That responsible task fell on you. Are congratulations in order?"

Propov seemed surprised, then broke into a roar of laughter. "Comrade Rublev, the honor is all yours."

"Mine?" Suddenly Vladi's brain was a thick maze of contradictory sentiments.

"Yes. Our boss needs feet on the ground in East Berlin, a

trustworthy man who will keep him informed about the situation there. Someone who isn't afraid to decide swiftly and act ruthlessly."

Coming from Propov's mouth, this was a compliment. Vladi prided himself in having no qualms to carry out Moscow's directives. This characteristic had earned him medals, a career, a comfortable life in the upper echelons of Soviet military. His only weakness was for beautiful women, whom he simply couldn't bring himself to mistreat. He left that part of the job to other colleagues who didn't feel the same aversion.

He fondly remembered Zara Ulbert, the daughter of a notorious SS-man and war criminal. She'd spent a couple of weeks in the caring hands of the NKVD, being tortured to inform on her father, but managed to resist the clueless bunglers, until Vladi had been tasked to finish the job.

His plan to loosen her tongue by giving her vodka, had backfired spectacularly. In the end the two of them had parted, if not exactly friends, at least respecting each other. And both of them had gotten what they wanted.

"I won't disappoint you."

"You'll be leaving for East Berlin in the morning."

Vladi bit his lip. He'd made plans with a very talented, very willowy ballet dancer from the Bolshoi theater. She'd be as disappointed as he was at having to abstain from a weekend full of fantastic sex. "Any directives I should follow while there?"

"Report to me once a week or when something important arises. Otherwise, align with Otto Grotewohl and Norbert Gentner. They don't have to take orders from you, so try to be diplomatic when telling them what to do."

"They shouldn't be a problem. It's in their best interest to work with me. After all, they called for our help." Vladi suppressed a smile. Diplomacy definitely wasn't his strength, yet he looked forward to verbal sparring matches with Rosalie.

"Don't indulge too much in luxuries over there; it's a temporary delegation." Propov wagged his finger. A posting to Berlin was highly coveted, since the living conditions in the German capital were so much better than in Moscow.

The next day, Vladi arrived at the Berlin airport. A chauffeur was waiting to take him to his lodgings in Karlshorst, where the high-ranking Soviet army members resided. He knew the area well from his three-year-stay in Berlin directly after Germany's capitulation in the Great Patriotic War.

"Colonel Rublev, welcome to Berlin. My name is Axel Becker, I'll be at your service throughout your stay." The tall, blond man was wearing the brown uniform of the National People's Army, the new East German army. He picked up Vladi's luggage and led him to a black Mercedes, presumably the seized property of a former Nazi bigwig.

As they drove through the city, Vladi noticed how much had changed in the past years. Pockmarked scars were still visible on the crumbling facades of buildings, and there were remnants of bombed-out structures. Yet, the heaps of rubble on the streets had vanished, cleared away by the famous *Trümmerfrauen*, hard-working housewives, who had shouldered the burden to rebuild their country. As they drove on, they passed several boroughs with newly erected rows of apartment buildings.

The driver seemed to notice Vladi's gaze in the rearview mirror and his face lit up with pride. "The entire residential area has been built in the last year. It's a quick and relatively inexpensive way of housing the many people who lost their homes in bombing raids, or relocated to Berlin from other areas." Relocation was very euphemistic for the brutal forced displacement of Germans living in regions further East, mainly East Prussia, Pomerania or the Sudetenland.

"How did they manage to build so many houses in such a short time?" Vladi was eager to know more, since the Soviet Union also suffered from a chronic housing shortage, even before the war.

"I'm not an engineer," Axel responded. "They way I understand it they use prefabricated concrete slabs, which slash the actual construction time to a few weeks at most. This method is used on all areas designated as *Neubaugebiet*, new development area."

"It is a clever way to advance your country."

"Yes, an apartment in one of the large-panel settlements is highly sought-after, because they offer modern amenities such as private indoor bathrooms, running hot water, electricity and central heating."

"It seems your country has already stepped into the prosperous future Marx promised to the workers and farmers after the revolution." Vladi ran a hand through his cropped hair in frustration, a pang of jealousy hitting him. The Soviet people had been promised paradise on earth for so long and his nation had been the first to start the Bolshevik revolution, yet living conditions for most citizens left a lot to be desired.

"Oh yes, our government is doing everything it can to improve the lives of our people." Axel must have noticed the sour expression on Vladi's face, because he quickly added, "Everyone in the country is grateful for the Soviet friendship. Without your help we would never have been able to achieve all of this."

Vladi seized the opportunity to get information about the current economic situation, which didn't come directly from the government itself. "So, why is there so much discontent amongst the population?"

Axel gave an exaggerated sigh. "It's disappointing, isn't it? People just don't seem to understand how good they have it."

"Unfortunately, the common people don't have the long-term vision our leaders do, and want immediate results. Though I am struggling to understand if there's any specific reason for the recent unrests."

Secretly Vladi thought the West had done a much better job at rebuilding their part of the country and improving the situation for their war-weary population. For obvious reasons, though, he never voiced his opinion.

"You know Comrade Gentner, don't you?" Axel asked, instead of elaborating on Vladi's words, which gave Vladi the impression that he must tread more carefully.

"I know him very well. He's doing a great job." Vladi leant

forward. "I've come here to assist your government with the current situation, and I'll be working closely with both Comrade Gentner and Comrade Grotewohl. To be better prepared I want to get an idea about the feeling on the street. Feel free to speak frankly. I'll know this is not your own opinion, it is merely your perception of what the common people are grappling with."

In his many years working for the Red Army Intelligence, he'd learned several strategies to receive answers. One of them was to reach a mutual understanding that any critique was not actually the interrogatee's opinion, but only what he had gathered from other anonymous people. As Vladi had expected, Axel's stiff jaw relaxed at the reassurance that he would not get into trouble for speaking up.

"Some people say the progress our socialist government has achieved is not fast enough. They look at the Imperialist West, deluded by their apparent wealth, while at the same time neglecting to see the high price those nations pay in the form of moral decay."

"Our system certainly is morally superior. What I'm trying to understand here is why people are suddenly voicing their discontent. Were there any specific triggers?" Once again, Vladi showed empathy to encourage an unguarded answer. "I absolutely understand that you're not an expert in these matters. Sometimes the experts are so involved in their topic they miss the forest for the trees, which is the very reason that I need an insight from someone on the ground, to get to the bottom of this."

"You may have heard about the government's aim to boost productivity and meet the demands of our socialist industrialization process?" Axel glanced into the mirror for a response. When Vladi nodded, he continued. "An increase in production quota and in working hours for factory employees was recently announced."

Vladi had known this already, yet he pretended this was news to him. "A challenging situation, indeed. It's unfortunate that the workers can't see the bigger picture and the long-term benefits of the socialist transformation."

"Most workers actually welcomed the increased quota, because they see the need for temporary sacrifices to rebuild our country.

However, this decision coincided with a drastic rise in the price of groceries, which caused a lot of discontent." Axel's face took on a miserable expression.

"It seems people continue to be shell-shocked from the years of hunger after the war." Vladi made a mental note to address food prices with Norbert. According to an old saying, a full belly wasn't prone to protest.

"Exactly, Comrade Rublev. The government's policies are part of a broader plan to implement socialism in our country. To combat the grocery price increases, they were forced to expropriate small farms in order to create large-scale collectives, following the model of the great Soviet Union." Axel stopped talking, focusing his attention on the traffic as he turned into another street.

"That should have helped right away. The efficiency gains of large collectives over parceled land are massive." Vladi repeated what he'd been taught for decades, not allowing his mind to make its own conclusions that nagged in the back of his head.

Axel scratched his clean-shaven chin. "Surprisingly it didn't. Nobody seems to know why, yet this agricultural shift resulted in a decline in output."

"It might take a while. Change is hard and such an ambitious project is bound to have teething troubles." Vladi caught a glimpse of another newly built large-panel settlement. The progress was undeniable, even the most conceited citizen had to realize that.

"Some people, and I absolutely don't agree with their point of view, insinuate that the private farms, albeit small, are superior in output over the collectives, because the owners have a personal investment in them."

Vladi inwardly shook his head. It was an old argument, which could easily be countered. "This happens only when people are not educated about the benefits of socialism. They tend to be greedy and prefer their individual wealth over their nation's well-being. In the Soviet Union we have overcome this pettiness by thorough re-education, starting in kindergarten." He made a mental note to also address the school system with Norbert. "The Soviet people have decades of advantage over the Germans. No doubt you'll catch up and, before you know it, your nation will pull together for the improvement of your country."

"We're fortunate to have the Soviet Union as a reliable friend and mentor." Axel steered the car onto the main street leading toward the Soviet Control Commission located in Karlshorst, which had replaced the Soviet Military Administration in Germany, a few years ago. "Should I drive you to the headquarters or do you want to go to your lodgings first?"

"Lodgings please, I have an appointment at the SCC later in the afternoon." Vladi relaxed against the seatback and gazed out the window, watching the familiar landscapes pass by. "Apart from the grocery prices and the increased quotas, what else aggrieves the common folk?"

"Well, some despicable elements have been trying to raise a crowd against the Soviet Union, falsely claiming that the reparations are the culprit of our economic woes."

Vladi had heard this grievance before. "The Imperialist West illegally stopped reparations to the Soviet Union, leaving the GDR to shoulder all mutual contractual obligations. Those people should be angry at the class enemy, not at our nation which has suffered immeasurably at the hands of the Germans. Yet we have still extended the hand of friendship." His voice had gradually risen with righteous anger at the ingratitude of certain elements of German society.

Seemingly believing the anger was directed toward himself, Axel shrank in the driver's seat until his head barely reached over the backrest. "Most of us, including me, condemn these subjects and want to see them rot in prison for the rest of their lives."

"It is incredibly useful to receive unfiltered news like you've given me. It helps me to be better prepared and to give your government adequate advice." Vladi needed to calm the waters if he ever wanted to use his driver as a source of information again. "Please accept my apology. I tend to get overly enraged at criminals and I shouldn't have directed my anger at you."

"No worries." Axel was visibly relieved to learn that he wasn't in trouble.

"I really appreciate your help. As I said before, Comrades Grotewohl and Gentner do a stellar job leading the nation, even though their elevated position makes it difficult for them to see what the common folks deal with. Therefore, I need you as my eyes and ears."

Axel beamed. "Thank you, Colonel Rublev, I'm happy to serve."

"The sacrifices made by the German people are necessary for the advancement of our shared socialist vision. I understand the hardships caused by these measures, nonetheless there is no way around it. Every one of us will be rewarded with a bright future."

"We have arrived, Colonel." Axel stopped in front of a row of nice detached houses, where the Soviet occupiers and the East German politicians lived.

"Thank you. Please pick me up again two hours from now."

"Of course. Is there anything else you might need?"

"Not at the moment." Vladi grabbed his suitcase and entered the house, which he was going to share with another military officer for the duration of his stay in Berlin.

Due to its separation into two countries, Germany dealt with an additional problem the other socialist countries didn't have. As austerity measures caused individual hardship, more and more citizens left the country for the relative prosperity of the West. Apart from speaking the same language, the escape was made easier by having relatives or friends in the Western zone. The mass exodus of mostly young, well-educated workers not only worsened the economic crisis, but also posed a threat to the stability of the socialist system.

Vladi would never have believed people could be as disloyal to their own leadership as the Germans were. Someday soon, the government would have to take harsh measures to impede its citizens from fleeing the republic.

CHAPTER 8

It was Friday night and Flori was about to go out on the town with her girlfriends, when Max, wearing dark pants and a long-sleeved blue shirt, arrived.

"Hello Max. Where are you headed in this fine attire?"

His face flushed a deep red. "Is Katja here?"

"So, you finally asked her out?" Flori couldn't suppress her grin.

"Umm, yes." It was a joy to watch his self-consciousness, since he was usually so composed.

"No, she hasn't arrived yet. She's with a friend, studying for her exams. That girl is too ambitious. She's already top of her class; what else does she want to achieve?"

"She wants to go to university." Max grimaced. "I'm so jealous. It's not that I begrudge her the opportunity, it's just that I also wanted very much to study, myself. And look at what has become of me?"

"You have an important job constructing housing." Flori often felt the same, having to give up her own aspirations to raise her sister. She absolutely wanted to see Katja succeed, yet it stung.

"Right…" His mouth turned down at the corners.

"Why so sullen?"

"It's difficult to remain happy when the country is steadily falling apart," Max responded miserably.

"Oh Max. It isn't half bad. We have enough to eat and a roof over our heads. That's a lot more than we had during the war."

"But in the last year or so, everything seems to have gone backwards. There's no more progress for us, the people. Every effort is concentrated on the heavy industries."

"This is only temporary; soon we'll see the fruits of our hard work." Flori harbored her own doubts, but now wasn't the time to voice them. Not because she didn't trust Max, but because she didn't know what exactly bothered her.

"I'm beginning to believe nothing's going to change for the better." Max ran a hand through his hair. "Nobody listens to us. The unions want to raise productivity, and they make plenty of suggestions of how to do it. None are implemented, and instead one stupid measure after another is announced. The politicians enrich themselves on the backs of the workers."

"That's not true..."

"Don't you see it yourself? They encourage us to suggest improvements, and when we do, they either ignore them or, even worse, jail the proponent for being a dissident."

"Now you're exaggerating." Deep inside she knew his words to be true, yet she would not acknowledge it even to herself, because that would open Pandora's box with so many more things to question. Her entire worldview would tumble to the ground if she allowed this to happen.

"You shouldn't talk like that." Flori instinctively hunched her shoulders, gazing around the apartment for listening ears. "Someone might report us to the Stasi and then we'll be in serious trouble."

"I rest my case," Max scoffed. "You're afraid to talk frankly in your own home."

Flori pressed her lips together to avoid arguing with him. Fortunately, in that moment, the door smashed open and Katja stomped inside.

"Hello Max, sorry for being late." Katja's eyes lit up, before disgust clouded them again.

"Problems at school?" Max asked, his face wearing a goofy smile, while his eyes devoured Katja.

Flori groaned inwardly at the obvious attraction between them, despite both of them fiercely denying any romantic interest in the other one.

"You can say that again. Those totalitarian bastards expelled two of my classmates from school for being a member of the Junge Gemeinde." Katja balled her hands into fists, looking as if she was about to punch someone.

"Was it that girl who was here a while ago? Liese?"

"Yes, her and Dirk."

"I told you to stay clear of her. Hopefully she won't cause you problems after all the effort it took to get you to where you are." Flori anxiously bit her lip. After some difficulties in the early years, strong-minded Katja had quickly adapted to the political situation and become an A-student, both education-wise and politically. She hadn't joined the SED, because she considered the party a "totalitarian shitshow" – her words, not Flori's – nonetheless she'd never publicly voiced a critical word against socialism, the party or any of the leaders. The girl was clever enough to understand how she needed to behave to advance in this country.

"Is that all you care about? What kind of soulless monster are you? How about showing some empathy for Liese and Dirk? Or at least pretend to?" Katja spat at her sister, her hands slamming up and down with rage.

"Katja, show some respect when talking to Flori. She sacrificed a lot to raise you." Max's sonorous voice rumbled through the small apartment. But even he couldn't calm Katja down.

"You expect me to overflow with gratitude for the rest of my life? I didn't ask Flori to sacrifice her dreams for me. It was her own choice."

"It was my choice and I don't expect you to be grateful forever, I just want you to not throw away everything in some reckless action." Flori knew her sister's rebellious temper, and especially her passion for justice.

"I'm sorry." Katja finally got a grip on her temper, her gaze fixed on the floor, unable to meet her sister's eyes. "There's more."

"Oh dear, what else?" A disturbing queasiness settled in Flori's stomach.

"I've been invited to a criticism and self-criticism session," Katja explained.

"You?" Max stared at her, incredulous. "I thought only party members were allowed to attend."

"Not if you're the one to be criticized."

"What did you do?" With wobbly knees, Flori walked the two steps over to the sofa.

"Nothing bad." A defiant glimmer appeared in Katja's eyes. "I merely stated that our constitution grants every citizen the freedom of religion. They didn't like that."

Max shook his head. "Ach Katja, don't tell me you genuinely believe we have the rights stipulated in the constitution. They're only granted where the party sees fit."

"Totalitarian shitshow," Katja mumbled beneath her breath. "I'm sick and tired of saying one thing and doing the other." She looked first at Max and then at Flori. "Both of you have told me many times over how bad the Nazis were. How is the SED any different?"

"Katja!" Flori gasped. "This incident might ruin your future."

"I know." Katja's mouth drooped at the corners. "I didn't plan this, it just happened. Liese never harmed anyone, she's the sweetest girl at school. When they accused her of being a terrorist, Western spy and whatnot, who's out to overthrow the GDR, I had enough and voted no to the expulsion."

Max raised an eyebrow. "That shouldn't warrant a session of criticism and self-criticism."

"Well...so this sorry excuse for a school director asked me why I had voted no. What was I supposed to say? I repeated what they've been hammering into me for the past few years: that we're a democratic country, in which the constitution stands above everything. I recited the article about freedom of religion and he didn't like it one bit." Katja pouted.

"When is your self-criticism?" Max asked.

"Monday."

"Want some advice?" When she nodded, Max explained how she should absolutely not plead guilty of anything at all and definitely not confess to criticizing the regime. Instead, she should wholeheartedly agree with party directives, admit that the Junge Gemeinde was a threat to society and that Liese had pulled the wool over her eyes.

"I'm not sure I can feign so much bigotry." Katja's eyes glared dangerously.

Flori knew how much her sister hated to put the blame on her friend. "Liese's future is lost anyway, not only because of her expulsion, but also because she openly admits to being a member of the Junge Gemeinde. Your career, though, can still be salvaged. Remember, your admission to university is at stake." Max took Katja's hand, his eyes locking with hers. Electricity passed between the two, so strong that Flori sensed it and suddenly felt like the third wheel.

"Am I disturbing you? I need to get going." Flori's voice was sharper than she'd intended because she fought against her jealousy. She didn't want Max for herself – he was like a brother to her – but she dearly wanted to fall in love with someone special, too. It wasn't fair that her little sister should have everything: a higher school education, her dream profession, and a wonderful man, while Flori got nothing except for long hours at the chocolate factory to make it all possible.

"Sorry." Max looked crestfallen. "Did I hold you up?"

"You've been doing that for hours." Flori smiled to take the sting out of her words.

"Every man will be running away if you go out dressed in that frumpy frock." Katja clapped her hands above her head.

"It's not like I have an entire wardrobe to choose from."

"Oh, come on. You make other women look like princesses with your fashion skills, and prefer to dress yourself like Cinderella?"

"Still waiting for the fairy godmother to conjure up a ball gown for me," Flori said dryly.

"You don't need a ball gown, a certain something will suffice." Katja's gaze searched the living room, until she focused on the bright-colored cloth adorning the sofa. She jumped up, took the cloth and draped it around her sister's shoulders like a shawl. "See? Much better."

"I'll have a look." Flori walked into the bathroom, climbing on top of a wooden box, which served as a makeshift stool, to scrutinize herself in the mirror above the sink. Then she took the shawl off her shoulders and slung it around her waist with a beautiful bow. The little trick transformed the sack-like frock into a tailored dress showcasing her slim waist and her bosom.

Perhaps Katja was right and the reason Flori hadn't found a man yet was because she had never even tried. On the spur of the moment, she decided this was going to change. Tonight, she'd make a splash. She combed her hair up into a bun and tied a broad ribbon around her head. Eyeing Katja's bright red lipstick, she borrowed it, smeared some color on her cheeks and then carefully painted her lips.

When she stepped out of the bathroom, Katja and Max sprung up like teenagers caught red-handed, her sister's cheeks tellingly rosy. Looking at her, both their jaws dropped to the floor.

"Stunning," Max mumbled, his eyes popping out of his head. "How did you do this?"

"You look phenomenal." Katja clapped her hands. "Now go out and catch that prince of yours."

"Katja. Stop it."

Katja grinned from ear to ear. "Wait one second." She disappeared into their bedroom and returned with a handbag she'd bought at a flea market. It was probably older than she was, which only added to its faded elegance. "Take this."

"Really?" Flori hesitated. "You'd loan it to me?"

"Sure. You're my big sister." Katja hung the handbag on her arm and stated in a satisfied tone, "Now you look like Grace Kelly." Then she embraced her and whispered in her ear, "You deserve to be happy."

"Thank you, sweetie." Flori hugged her back, realizing she had stopped being a mother and Katja was no longer the child.

When she met her friends at the underground station, Klara gasped at the sight of her and asked in mock surprise, "Who are you? And what have you done to our Flori?"

"Katja dolled me up. Is it too brash?" Flori certainly didn't want to look like a lady of the night.

"Not at all. The ugly duckling has turned into a swan, truly a stunning transformation." Klara whistled through her teeth.

"Can Katja do the same to me next time?" Helga asked, as they took the underground train to the American sector, where the best bars were located. They had all saved up money and changed their Ostmark into the much higher valued Westmark, which was the main reason why they so rarely ventured into the other sectors. Due to the currency exchange, it was prohibitively expensive.

When they arrived at the bar, several posh women were dancing with American soldiers. Flori and her friends simultaneously envied, and looked down on them, for hooking up with the foreigners. Some might be truly in love; most women, though, exchanged intimacies for nylons, lipstick, and cigarettes.

Living in the Soviet sector of Berlin, they were allowed to move freely through all sectors of the city. However, dating an American soldier was completely out of the question. Any East Berlin woman caught with the enemy – and all Western soldiers were considered enemies – might face interrogation and punishment. She could be accused of anything ranging from treason to espionage, and be shipped to Siberia to disappear forever.

A shudder racked Flori's shoulders. Even if she didn't have moral qualms about dating an American or Brit, she'd never risk it. In contrast, dating a Soviet soldier wasn't exactly encouraged, but not forbidden either. Another shudder raced through her bones; she'd rather cut off her arms than date a Soviet, too painful were the memories of the abuse she'd suffered at their hands – or more precisely, other body parts – shortly after the war.

Some women seemed to have a shorter memory, or had been luckier. They weren't well-liked by their peers, and Russian slut was the mildest cuss hurled at them. Per party directive, the Soviets were the friends, saviors and benefactors of the German people. In reality, though, not many seemed to like them.

"Too bad that Carolin couldn't make it, husband problems or some such rubbish!" Klara was always outspoken. "That man really bosses her around. I don't know how she stands it."

"She loves him. He's a good husband to her and a good father to the children." Flori fiddled with her bun, making sure the ribbon bow was still in place.

"To each his own, I suppose. I would never tolerate a man telling me what to do." If born earlier, she would have, no doubt, joined the suffragette movement.

"Which is why you're still single," Helga replied.

Else met up with them in front of the bar, because she'd recently moved in with her cousin in the American sector. "This is my cousin - Marlene Kupfer." She pointed at a slim, tall brunette next to her. "Are you alright if she joins us tonight?"

"Welcome." Flori extended her hand to make the introductions. Marlene was four years older than Flori and worked as a lawyer for the Americans. She looked absolutely stunning in her polka-dotted red dress, which Flori recognized as being from the famous Kaufhaus des Westens, located in the American sector. The famous department store, nicknamed KaDeWe, had been reopened just three years ago after undergoing a massive reconstruction. Western media outlets celebrated it as a *symbol of the German economic miracle* and the epitome of the *free West* in the frontline city of Berlin.

Political issues aside, Flori would have loved to shop in the posh store, if it weren't unaffordable for her due to it only accepting

Westmark. Still, she often passed by to window shop and get ideas she could use for the dresses she designed for friends on the side.

They found a cozy corner that provided them with a vantage point to observe the comings and goings of the patrons, and ordered beer. Soon enough, the rhythmic music dissolved the stress of the workweek and Flori joined her friends on the dance floor.

CHAPTER 9

Vladi had spent all day in meetings with Norbert Gentner and the labour minister. Otto Grotewohl, the prime minister, had joined them for the first hour, before he had excused himself to attend other government business.

Vladi welcomed the prime minister's exit. He and Norbert were on the same wavelength, whereas Grotewohl abhorred Vladi's unconventional methods.

Vladi returned to his lodgings, to change his uniform for civvies. He wanted to look like an ordinary citizen, because most women, especially the pretty ones, disliked a Soviet soldier. He couldn't blame them after what had happened directly after the war. It had been a disgusting free-for-all with the German Fräuleins being the spoils on offer.

Personally, he much preferred a pliable, willing woman for his nightly activities and, due to his bad boy charm, there had never been a shortage of those, even during the free-for-all period in 1945. The more street-smart girls had quickly realized that giving themselves voluntarily to one Soviet soldier – the higher ranking the better – protected them from being violated by many.

Walking into the detached house, he found his roommate sitting on the sofa, reading the Moscow newspaper *Prawda*.

He greeted the impeccably-dressed captain with a curt nod. "Comrade Zhukov."

Judging by the younger man's slicked-back dark hair, the clean-shaven face and the uniform, which looked freshly pressed even after a day's work, Captain Zhukov was a career soldier, much too young to have seen action during the Great Patriotic War.

He wasn't the kind of guy Vladi would usually hang out with. But in the absence of a better alternative, he decided not to be selective.

"Colonel Rublev." Zhukov put his newspaper aside to jump to attention.

After returning the salute, Vladi said, "Since we're going to share this house, I think we can dispense with the formalities, for the time being." The stiff expression on Zhukov's face kept Vladi from offering to be on a first name basis. The man didn't seem comfortable with anything but formality with a superior officer.

This caused Vladi to reconsider his plan to hit the bars with his colleague. "Please, no saluting while we're inside the house."

"Yes, Colonel Rublev." Zhukov's hand twitched upward before he caught himself and stood ramrod straight.

"At ease." Even as Vladi wondered if the straightlaced lad would know any of the hot bars in Berlin, he said, "I was wondering if you could recommend a popular bar in town."

By the way Zhukov fought to prevent his face turning into a grimace, Vladi already knew the answer.

"I'm normally too busy, but on Friday night I sometimes go to a bar in the Karlshorst barracks."

"Thank you very much for your suggestion." Vladi inwardly recoiled with disgust. He certainly had no intention of spending his time with ambitious career soldiers, looking as if someone had rammed a rod up their ass.

He retired to his room, where he stepped out of his uniform to take a refreshing shower and then dressed in his beloved black pants, dark shirt and leather jacket. To complete the going-out look, he carefully tousled his cropped ash-blond hair in just the style he knew women found attractive.

When Axel arrived to collect him, he didn't seem surprised to see Vladi had changed out of his uniform. "I reckon you want to blend in?"

"I sure do. I want to chat to ordinary folks about the current situation." Actually, that was not the main reason. Finding a female companion for a night – or longer – was his real agenda.

"Axel, can you recommend some hot bars in town?"

"I certainly know of a few. Although, if you want to get a clear picture on the kind of people who oppose the government's directives, you'll have to visit the bars in the Western sectors." Axel held open the back door for Vladi to step into the limousine.

Vladi knew from experience that the bars in the West were a thousand times better than the ones in the East. However, without knowing how close Axel toed the party line, he wasn't going to admit to this, so he said, "The opinions of West Berliners are of no importance to me or the GDR government. Their main goal is to destroy the morally superior socialism."

"Unfortunately, many East Berliners, especially those who are discontented with one measure or the other, frequent the Western Sectors at night." Axel settled behind the wheel and started the motor.

"Well then. I might have to bite the bullet." It was the perfect cover for Vladi's own plans. He thought for a few seconds before he asked about his favorite place. "Does the Café de Paris still exist?"

"Doesn't ring a bell."

"It belonged to Herr Schuster and used to be the best cabaret in town." Vladi held fond memories of its many peachy waitresses, and of the entertainer, the gorgeous platinum-blonde singer Bruni von Sinnen – not that she'd ever let him into her bed. She was way out of his league, having been the semi-official lover of Feodor Orlvoski, the man in charge of the Soviet technical corps, before she'd exchanged him for Dean Harris, the American Commandant in Berlin.

Bruni was not only exceptionally talented and beautiful, but also knew how to take advantage of her allure. He admired her immensely for that. The Café de Paris had been her springboard to fame and fortune: she now lived in America, idolized by the masses, Broadway and Hollywood.

Axel interrupted his musings. "Oh, I know the one. It closed several years ago. There was a huge scandal. The owner Herr Schuster was involved in a big-time smuggling ring, which was said to have sold jewels, precious metals and art stolen by the Nazis with a total value of several million US dollars, to foreign countries."

Vladi raised an eyebrow. Despite keeping up to date with international news, this bit of information had never made it into the newspapers he read. "Well then, what bar do you recommend?"

Axel turned around, a slightly sheepish expression on his face. "I've never gone there myself, however *The Liberty Lounge* has a certain fame among partying night owls."

"Sounds perfect. Let's go there." It was typical of the Americans to choose such a flashy name. They never missed an opportunity to draw attention to their exaggerated patriotism and false understanding of freedom.

"I'm sorry, I won't be able to drive you all the way. We're not allowed to cross the sector borders on official business."

"Oh, right." That measure had been installed during the traffic restrictions in 1948, stubbornly called *Blockade* by the Western Allies to justify their silly air circus, when everyone knew it was nothing but a ruse to show off their war planes for sale to the highest bidder.

"I can drive you all the way to the Brandenburger Tor. There you cross over on foot like any other Berliner. Since you're out of uniform, and your German is fluent, nobody will ask for your papers."

"Thank you for your advice. That sounds like a valid plan." Vladi winked at Axel, having gained the impression the man wasn't just talking from hearsay.

Near the Brandenburger Tor, Axel stopped the vehicle. "Shall I wait for you?"

"No need. I'll find my own way back home." *Or into the home of a willing woman.* "I'll see you in the morning to drive me to Marx-

Engels-Platz, where I'm going to have a meeting with the Politburo."
Then he turned on his heels and disappeared into the American
sector. Here, the city had progressed even more in the years since
Vladi's departure to Moscow.

He found *The Liberty Lounge* right away. It possessed exactly the
ambience he'd hoped for. The rhythmic music immediately cast a
spell on him, as did the posh crowd of partygoers, through which
waitresses wove, their trays full of drinks. It was a merry atmosphere
fizzing with optimism.

Making his way through the crowd, his gaze fell on a dancing
woman. She was surrounded by what seemed to be her clique of
girlfriends. Mesmerized, he stared at her. The red, polka-dotted
dress itself couldn't compare to the elegant gowns of Moscow's
famous actresses and ballet dancers, but the colorful waistbelt made
it into a piece of art, enhancing the beauty of the slim woman
wearing it.

She twirled around, her eyes locking with his for a moment,
sending a hot flash into his groin. Never had a woman's gaze
impacted him like this. A lazy smile spread across his lips as
exhilaration coursed through his veins. This beauty was the lucky
chosen one to experience pure bliss in his arms tonight – she just
didn't know it yet.

The music changed to the smooth tones of a saxophone,
accompanied by the gentle tinkle of a grand piano. Most dancers
used it as an excuse to return to their tables to have a drink and
recoup their energy.

Vladi kept his gaze on the woman he'd set his eyes on. When she
and her friends walked toward the bathrooms, he put his tried and
tested plan into motion, positioning himself at the bar, where she
would have to pass on her way back.

Chasing a woman wasn't so different from observing a suspect.
Out of habit, his eyes scanned the room, taking in every small detail.
The grand bar that stretched across the length, showed some of its
pre-war splendor despite scratches and stains marring the finish.
Glistening crystal glasses and bottles of top-shelf liquor, no doubt

reserved for the American soldiers paying in hard dollars, filled the shelves behind the bar.

Several uniformed men stood engrossed with German Fräuleins in animated conversation or heated embraces. He licked his lips in anticipation; this place was a perfect hunting ground indeed. Given his flawless track record, he estimated how much time it would take to get her lips on his, then have her hand on his arm on the way to her place, as being less than an hour.

Patiently waiting, he wondered what her story was. Every German, male or female, had a sad story to tell after more than a decade of fascism, six years of war and eight years of occupation.

Due to his work in the Red Army Intelligence, he loved finding out the motivation behind the actions of a human being. Once he knew this, he was able to extract information from the person. Even the most resilient ones, like Zara Ulbert who'd withstood weeks of NKVD torture, had ultimately given him what he wanted, without him ever having to lay a hand on her.

Vladi was certainly no saint and enjoyed a good old-fashioned beating up more than he should – if the victim was a man. He drew the line at hurting a woman, much to General Propov's chagrin, who often accused him of being too soft.

When she stepped out of the ladies' room, Vladi's heart fluttered in a very unexpected way. Close up, she looked even more alluring. Her face was fresh and innocent, and her posture showed an inner confidence.

He waited for the perfect moment to step in front of her. Their eyes locked and time stood still for an instant. The strong connection caught him completely unawares, making it incredibly hard to refrain from taking her into his arms right there and then.

Suddenly, his firm emotional control melted under a wave of tenderness, as he became lost in the depths of her hazel eyes. Warmth spread from his heart throughout his body, letting him momentarily forget his rehearsed advances. In the midst of the lively bar, a gentle silence seemed to envelop them, their surroundings fading into the background. The noise and chatter became a mere murmur, drowned out by the rush and intensity of their connection. In that split-second, it seemed as if he had waited for her throughout his entire lifetime. Judging by the enthralled expression in her eyes, she experienced the same sensations.

Vladi had never believed in love at first sight, or rather, love at all, because it defied logic and reason. Now, he wasn't sure what to believe. He didn't know how much time ticked by before he found the strength to break the spell, taking a hesitant step toward the most wonderful woman on earth, his eyes never leaving hers.

"Vladimir Rublev at your service, pretty Fräulein," he said, taking her hand to bestow a kiss on it. "Please allow me to buy you a drink."

"Thank you for your invitation, *mein Herr*, but I'm here with friends." She was about to turn around and walk away. It took him a quarter of a second to recover – he'd never been rebuffed before. His brain went into overdrive to find a solution to his predicament. He absolutely had to get to know this woman, if only to discover why she'd refused when she was so obviously attracted to him.

"In that case, your friends are obviously invited, too." He gave her the often-practiced smile, which women usually found irresistible.

"All five of them?" she queried, rolling her eyes.

His expense account wasn't as generous as before the currency reform, when the SMAD had enjoyed virtually unlimited access to funds, since it could always print more money. He nodded regardless, fully expecting her to agree. "If it means I can chat with you for a few minutes, then yes."

"I can't possibly accept your offer." Her sweet, yet firm answer surprised him very much, because he possessed enough experience with women to notice the arousal in her dilated eyes. What was wrong with her?

He wouldn't be Vladimir Rublev though, if he gave up at the first obstacle. While he pondered his next move, he received unexpected support when one of her girlfriends approached them.

"Where have you been, Flori?" The feisty brunette stopped in her tracks when she noticed him, gave him the once-over, signaled approval to Flori, then extended her hand. "I'm Klara Gundel, Floriane's friend."

"It's a pleasure to meet you Fräulein Klara, I'm Vladimir Rublev. I have invited your friend for a drink."

"And I was about to tell him that we are leaving," Floriane said.

Vladi let her name silently roll over his tongue, savoring the sensations it evoked in him. It was such a fitting name for this stunning woman. It derived from the Roman name Florianus or Florus and translated as "the blossoming", "the magnificent" or "the wonderful", all three fitting descriptions for the beauty standing in front of him, in spite of the scowl on her face.

Klara didn't seem to notice Floriane's glare and protested, "It's not even midnight, Flori. Why don't you come to sit at our table with us, Herr Rublev?"

"I don't want to intrude," he hedged politely, fully aware that Klara wouldn't let him leave so easily, which suited his plan.

"You won't intrude at all. We're a group of girls having a night out." Klara linked arms with him and dragged him behind her to their table. On any other occasion he would have flirted with her; tonight, however, his sights were set solely on Floriane. Klara introduced him to Helga, Else and Marlene. The latter seemed faintly familiar, though he couldn't quite place her.

"I'm Vladimir Rublev, but please call me Vladi." He hoped his German was still as fluent as it had been a few years ago, since he didn't want anyone to know he belonged to the Soviet Army. Flori reluctantly settled next to him, as Klara pushed them onto the bench.

He ordered a bottle of wine for the table. With Floriane near enough to touch, heat flared up in his body. He inwardly shook his head – never before had a woman filled him with such fiery desire. Right now, all he wanted to do was to take her home with him and never let her go again for the rest of their lives.

"Vladi, how come you have a Russian name?" There was a little hostility in Floriane's voice.

He'd been expecting the question and used the backstory he'd made up before when needing to explain his Russian accent, which couldn't be further from the truth. "My mother married a Russian. When he died, we returned to live with her family in Germany."

"I'm sorry." It was Helga who sent him a sympathetic smile, whereas Klara cocked her head, batting her eyelashes at him.

"It was a long time ago." He bestowed a measured smile on her, before he turned his attention toward Floriane, giving her the full-on, charming grin he'd perfected in many years of talking women round. "How about you, what are you doing for the rest of the night?"

"Having fun with my friends," she quipped, which made him admire her even more. True, it was a nuisance that she fought her obvious attraction to him instead of instantly falling into his arms. On the other hand, it made the chase so much more thrilling, relentlessly pumping adrenaline through his veins and heightening his senses. It would be magnificently rewarding to finally carry her into his bed.

The women playing hard-to-get usually fell into two categories: those who genuinely believed in chastity until after matrimony and those who enjoyed the game as much as he did. The first category was to be avoided like the plague, the second one though...pure dynamite. Floriane appeared to belong to the latter.

"What do you do for a living?" asked Marlene, who hadn't talked much so far. The way she scrutinized his face made the hair on his neck stand on end. Intuitively he guessed she was probing his background story. Did she remember him from his previous stay in Berlin?

"I'm a commercial agent." He deliberately didn't offer any detail.

"How interesting. May I ask for whom?" Marlene's expression was innocent enough, but it still gave him the chills.

"Certainly. It's not a secret. I'm in the business of construction machines." This was a topic which women usually rolled their eyes at in boredom and quickly changed the subject. He'd once made the mistake of claiming to work in a shoe factory. A criticism and self-criticism session was preferable to being quizzed by a bunch of women about everything to do with shoes, when all he knew about them was to distinguish size and color.

"How interesting," Elsa said, in a tone that clearly indicated she found the topic extremely tedious.

"Let's not talk about me. What do you do for a living?"

"We're working in a chocolate factory."

"Now that sounds interesting to me. Such sweet girls working with sweets." It was a bit cheesy, but the best he could come up with on the spur of the moment.

Else and Klara giggled, while Floriane rolled her eyes at him. "Now, that is a stupid remark if ever I heard one. Do you think we roll in chocolate all day?"

The question conjured up images of her naked body covered in delicious chocolate sauce and him licking it off. He swallowed hard, willing his mind to behave. The fun part would have to wait until later; first he had to woo her.

"I'm sorry, that was indeed a stupid thing to say." He raised his hands, gazing deep into her wonderful eyes. Powerful charges of energy sprang between them, the jolt reaching all the way down into his loins. "I don't know anything about the chocolate- making process and would love to hear more about it."

As he'd expected, his admission of fault softened Floriane's resistance. Her mouth lost its hardness, the corners of her lips tugging upwards into an almost-smile. *Not quite there yet, but she's warming up.*

All the women, except for Marlene, talked over each other as they eagerly explained the steps in chocolate production from the cocoa bean to the finished product. He would never again be able to put a piece of the sweet into his mouth without remembering this lively scene.

"We are going to miss the last train if we don't leave now." Flori gave her friends a steady look that asked them not to argue.

"Shall I…" Vladi stopped himself before asking if he should call his driver, which he usually did, in equal parts to impress his newest fling and to make sure she arrived home safely. "…accompany you to the underground station?"

"No need. There's three of us," Helga said.

"And fortunately, the Soviet soldiers have since learned to behave," Floriane added, her glare daring him to defend them.

"Indeed, the situation has changed considerably – for the better I may say." He turned to look at Marlene and Else. "What about you?"

"We live in the American sector, where the Soviets have no say." Marlene gave him a knowing smirk, which again caused his neck hair to stand on end. This woman knew, or at least suspected, he hadn't told them the truth about his origin.

The discomfort about her suspicion was so strong, he barely registered the insult against his kin. Admittedly, he personally hadn't condoned the way his compatriots had behaved after the conquest, but what had the Germans expected after killing, torturing, raping, and looting the Soviet population for years? Kindness? Friendship? Consideration?

As they left the bar, Vladi seized the opportunity to take Floriane's hand. "I have enjoyed your company immensely. May I please see you again?"

The expressions crossing her face betrayed her inner conflict. At last she answered, "You already know where I work. Next week my shift ends at four p.m."

Given her earlier reluctance, this was a much better outcome than he'd expected. "I'll be there. Have a good night, Floriane."

"You too, Vladi."

CHAPTER 10

S tomach cramps made it impossible to eat breakfast. Floriane had left for work and Katja was alone at home, trying to muster the courage to pack her satchel and walk to school to face her criticism and self-criticism session.

Every one of her classmates who'd attended such a session, even those who hadn't been the accused, had come out of it a very strong shade of pale. The "culprits" were always shaken to the core and often hadn't returned to school.

Somehow she managed to trudge up the stairs to the director's office, where some of her classmates – all of them party members – were waiting. Looking at the severe faces around her, she knew she was in serious trouble.

Regret bubbled up inside her. Defending Liese hadn't helped her friend, it had only served to get Katja into dire straits. Perhaps, if she agreed to any of the stupid charges of defending the Junge Gemeinde and also reneged on citing the constitution - which everyone knew wasn't worth the paper it was written on - nothing bad would happen to her.

Max had counseled her to forget Liese for the moment and try to save herself, since it was her future at stake. He begged her to denounce her ideological errors and pledge allegiance to the party line. Swallowing her pride and righteous indignation, she'd promised to do that. She would agree to anything and everything if it meant she was still allowed to study at the prestigious Humboldt University.

"Friendship," announced the principal as he opened the session. In front of him lay a long list, presumably of Katja's many crimes and shortcomings.

"Friendship," the students responded.

"Comrades," the principal's loud and stern voice boomed, "we are here today to expose and correct the serious faults of our student, Katja Eilers. As you all witnessed last week, she has betrayed the socialist cause, denigrated the workers' movement, and put our glorious leaders to shame. She has been influenced by the imperialist propaganda of the West, and she has fallen prey to the reactionary ideology of religion. She has shown disrespect to her teachers, her classmates, and her country. We're here to give her a chance to become a better person by purging herself of these malevolent influences."

He paused, looking at each student to let the gravity of Katja's crimes sink in. Lastly, he fixed his gaze on her. "Katja Eilers, do you have anything to say for yourself?"

Katja valiantly fought against the tears pooling in her eyes. "I am sorry."

"Apologizing is a laudable first step." His voice had lost a sliver of its ice. "If you truly repent, the party will welcome you into her midst again, giving you the opportunity to become a valuable community member once more."

Anger snaked up her spine as she watched her puppet-like classmates, voicelessly repeating the principal's words with their lips. When had she stopped being a valuable person? When she'd defended a friend? When she'd repeated what the politics teacher had drilled into her for years? Or when she'd taken the words of her government at face value?

"But first we must bring all your flaws into the open. Exposing them will help you to free yourself of damaging influences, to shed everything that is bad inside you, so that you may rise from the ashes a new and better person. Who wants to begin?"

Unsure what was about to happen, Katja looked at Frank, who quickly turned his head aside. The stomach cramps returned out of the blue. She fought the urge to double over. This session was much worse than she'd expected.

Marga walked toward the blackboard and said, "You are stubborn and arrogant. You are deluded and ignorant. You are ungrateful and rebellious. You are a disgrace to this school and this nation."

"Thank you." The principal dismissed Marga with a wave of his hand and she returned to her seat.

One by one, everyone in the room stood up and hurled insults and accusations at Katja.

"You are a bad student," said one of her teachers. "You never pay attention in class, you never do your homework, you never participate in extracurricular activities. You are lazy and incompetent."

"Katja, you are a bad friend," said one of her classmates. "You never help us with our problems, you never share your things with us, you never join us in our fun. You are selfish and greedy."

"Katja, you are a bad citizen," said another. "You never respect the laws, you never support the party, you never love your country. You are disloyal and treacherous."

Despite knowing deep in her heart that none of these outrageous accusations were true, pain over the betrayal of her classmates threatened to suffocate her. The urge to lash out and yell at this humiliating farce, became so overwhelming she had to bite her tongue. Over and over she repeated in her head: *This is not true. Stay calm and pretend to agree with everything they say. Think of university.*

As the onslaught of denigration continued, she searched the faces of the people she had considered her friends – no one dared to meet her eyes, for fear of being the next victim in this vicious charade. With sudden clarity she realized that they were doing exactly what Max had advised her to do: save themselves rather than speak up on a friend's behalf.

If she succumbed now, this would be her life forever: cowing to an unjust authority. Katja swallowed the lump forming in her throat, raising her chin. No, she would not grovel. Neither would she keep her mouth shut when fascism again raised its ugly head.

Finally, it was her turn to speak. Eager faces expected to hear her admission of guilt. Wanted to see her squirm admitting an imaginary guilt, to renounce everything she believed in and to beg for forgiveness for a crime she had not committed.

Oh yes, they wanted her to show remorse, humility, and gratitude to the party, the nation and its people.

But she wasn't about to do that. To hell with the consequences. She stood up and slowly walked toward the blackboard, where she turned to face the withering looks of her henchmen.

"Comrades." She took a deep breath, mustering the courage required to speak up. "I am not sorry for defending my friend, Liese. I believe in law and order and, above all, I want to believe in the rights given to every German citizen as stipulated in our constitution. If staying in your midst requires me to value lies over truth, violence over peace, hate over love, then I'm afraid I cannot do that." She looked at them with a calm confidence. "I am not a traitor or a revisionist or a bourgeois sympathizer. I merely want to be a free person with the freedom to speak my mind."

A stunned silence filled the room. No one knew how to react or what to do next. Never before had an accused reacted in such an unexpected way.

Her head held high, Katja walked through the door, possibly for the last time in her life, since her defiance of the status quo would never be allowed. When the door clicked shut behind her, she knew for certain that she had just sealed her fate.

But she also knew she had just won back her soul.

CHAPTER 11

W hen Max returned home after work, he found a shivering Katja crouching in front of his apartment door.

"Katja, dear, what are you doing here?" He immediately suspected the criticism and self-criticism session had gone awry.

"Can I come in, please?" She sniffed. Despite her puffy face, swollen from crying, she was the most beautiful woman in the world. She'd been like a little sister to him for most of her life, until about two years ago, when he'd started to develop feelings, which had been confusing to say the least.

"Coffee?" At her nod, he disappeared into the kitchen to brew *Muckefuck*, which tasted similar to real coffee, but was made mostly from grain with an addition of chicory to give it a bitter note. When he returned, Katja was sitting on the sofa, her arms wrapped around her knees.

"Here you go." He handed her a mug. "Now, tell me what has you so upset."

"They expelled me from school." She sniffed again.

"Why?"

"I basically told them to shove their bigotry up their behinds."

Max took a deep breath to keep himself from saying something he might later regret. "They probably didn't like that."

She snorted. "That's the understatement of the century. After I walked out the door, the principal followed me, shouting like a maniac and banning me from ever setting foot on the school grounds again."

He settled next to her, putting an arm around her shoulders, to which she reacted by leaning against him.

"What am I going to do?" Sobs shook her upper body.

"You should have thought about that before contradicting the principal in front of however many party members." Her grief tucked at Max's heart, yet he needed to point out that her own actions had gotten her into this plight.

"I know. But it...it just...the whole system is so unjust. They always say one thing and do another."

Max gave a heartfelt sigh; he'd been feeling the same way for a while now. After the capitulation, he had been full of hope for a better future, as promised by the socialist government. Nowadays though...all optimism had dissipated. The same government that promised to work for the interests of the common people, issued policies that made life harder. They diverted resources to heavy industry, neglecting agriculture and production of consumer goods, while promising the people jam tomorrow.

Eight years after the capitulation, the economy hadn't improved all that much. The Western zones thrived while the East buckled under the burden of reparations, continually fighting against the wind.

"Regardless, you should have concentrated on getting your diploma, instead of agitating. Sometimes one must put up with injustice, at least for a while."

"That's rich coming from you! You became a union leader so you could fight for the workers' rights!"

"It's entirely different, Katja. My job is to work as part of the system, not against it." Max stroked her shoulder. "Don't you think I want to chuck it all in sometimes, too?"

"You do?" Her eyes searched his, revealing her surprise.

"Sure. There are so many problems in our country and the union members often have good proposals to solve them, but nobody listens to us."

"Don't you meet with government officials all the time?"

He cast her a wry smile. "We do. We talk. And then they go and continue on the same path as before. We may as well talk to a wall."

"Have you ever..." She furrowed her brows, looking around the tiny apartment, before she continued to speak in a low voice, "... considered leaving the country?"

"I'd never receive permission, because my job is vital for the country's economy. And leaving the republic without permission is illegal."

"Why do they even want to keep us here, if they don't allow us to pursue the career we want? Or finish high school?" Katja jumped up, a rebellious glint in her eyes.

"I honestly don't know. All I can say is that it is what it is and we can only change things from within. So you better find a way to return to school and graduate. Then you can go to university, become an engineer, join a union and work to improve things."

Katja's eyes had become bigger and bigger during his little speech. "By then I'll be old and doddery. I'm sick and tired of being cajoled with a future that will most probably never materialize."

She voiced what Max had secretly been thinking himself, and what he didn't have a solution for. "What are you planning to do instead?"

"I don't know yet. I'll find something." Her face fell. "You're not going to tell Flori, are you?"

"I cannot lie to her," he replied. "If she asks me, I'll have to come clean."

"But you won't broach the topic yourself, please?" She looked at him with such pleading eyes, he couldn't deny her the wish.

"Alright. I won't say anything, except if she asks."

"Thank you so much." Katja fell around his neck, hugging him tight.

They'd been twice on a date, however he hadn't yet dared to kiss her. Now that her soft and warm body pressed against him, he couldn't resist any longer and took her face between his hands.

"My sweet darling, may I kiss you?"

Instead of an answer, she went onto her tiptoes, offering her slightly opened lips to him. Butterflies somersaulted in his stomach as he lowered his head, pressing his mouth onto hers.

"That was very nice," she said, her face flushed. "May I have another one?"

With a happy chuckle, he bent to match her height. While their first kiss had been careful and gentle, this time he didn't hold back and pushed his tongue through her lips, exploring every nook and cranny of her mouth, savoring her taste and the wonderful feeling of being so close to her. It evoked powerful sensations across his entire body and deep into his loins.

Panting heavily, they finally came up for air, gazing at each other in wonder.

CHAPTER 12

Norbert Gentner sat in his hotel room with Rosalie. They were part of a delegation summoned to Moscow. After Stalin's death, events had followed in quick succession, coming to a head when the very existence of the young German Democratic Republic was at stake, due to a severe food crisis.

For some reason, the collectivization of land had not resulted in the expected improvements in efficiency and increased production – leading to discontent among the general population, and especially the farmers, craftsmen, self-employed and retailers, who'd been heavily taxed as well as excluded from the ration coupon system for food, clothing and domestic fuel.

Add unfavorable weather to that and the situation was dire. No crop was produced in sufficient quantities to feed the population; long queues in front of stores were an ubiquitous sight. Even the generous support provided by the Soviet Union wasn't enough to make a difference.

People were sick and tired of the living conditions and voted with their feet, fleeing the GDR for greener pastures in West Germany. Norbert pressed his jaws together. The mass exodus posed an economic as well as a social threat, since mostly the young and well-educated left.

"We can't allow everyone to up and leave," he mumbled.

Rosalie was sitting next to him and put a hand over his. "I've been thinking about this, too. If people don't see reason, we might have to nudge them in the right direction."

"How should we do this?" Warmth spread throughout his body as he observed his wife, knowing she understood him without words. She was truly his best asset.

"Close the borders."

"We've already done that. It's illegal to leave the country without a permit." He bit his lip, pondering the problem.

"Which doesn't deter most of the subjects willing to flee," Rosalie said, snuggling up against him. "You need to physically close the border."

"Hmm." He pensively rubbed his chin. "We've established restricted zones around the border stations, which no one is allowed to freely enter. However, we can't possibly place guards along the entire one thousand four hundred kilometers of the demarcation line."

Rosalie scrunched her nose. "There must be hundreds of thousands of mines and grenades left over from the war. Instead of destroying them, wouldn't it be beneficial if you put them to a better use?" She looked up at him, excitement glimmering in her eyes. "An antifascist barrier to protect our nation from the evil influence."

"To keep the class enemy out and our citizens in?" Norbert immediately saw the benefit in her idea. "It's genius! You're a genius!"

"Thank you, my darling." Her smile lit up the hotel room. "It will be like the mythical river Styx that can only be crossed with the help of Charon, the ferryman of the dead. A frontier separating the living from the dead."

"Don't get overly excited." He kissed her temple. "It will take years of hard work to convert the demarcation line into a tightly-sealed death strip."

"If anyone can do it, it will be you." Rosalie wrapped her arms around him. "I love you so much."

He chuckled and, after a quick glance at his wristwatch, swept her up in his arms, and strode toward their bed.

"Hey, what are you doing? We have to get ready for our meeting with the Political Counselor Wladimir Semjonov," she protested, laughing.

"Then we better make it real quick."

~

About an hour later, they arrived at the Kremlin in time for their meeting with Semjonov.

"Comrade Semjonov, thank you so much for meeting with us." Norbert gave Semjonov a socialist fraternal kiss on the mouth to express the unbreakable friendship between their countries.

"Welcome to Moscow." Semjonov turned toward Rosalie, embracing her and kissing her three times on alternate cheeks. "Have you had a pleasant trip?"

"It was smooth as always. By the way, the hotel room you arranged for us is absolutely delightful. I must say, Moscow does have the best hotels in the world." Rosalie cast a bright smile at the man, whom she knew to be susceptible to female flattery.

He bowed his head with delight. "I hope our visit tonight to the Bolshoi theatre will elicit the same praise from you."

"I'm certain it will. I am eagerly looking forward to yet another highlight of Soviet culture." She put a suggestive hand on Semjonov's arm.

From a few steps away, Norbert observed how Rosalie expertly played the man who held the power over their political future. Having to watch his wife flirt with the Political Counselor was a small price to pay for the support he was able to extend. It wouldn't be her first time either, at sneaking out of the hotel room to intensify the relationship with an important decision maker. As long as she returned with forged alliances in the morning, Norbert didn't mind.

A rap on the door interrupted them and Semjonov clapped his

hands. "Business before pleasure. I have allowed myself to invite our economic experts to attend our discussion of rather delicate matters."

"I am eager to hear your suggestions." Norbert had done well listening to Soviet directives, or advice as they liked to call it, and swiftly implementing it to the letter.

"Come in," Semjonov boomed. Seconds later, the economic expert entered; a young man in his early thirties, no doubt an elite graduate of the Lomonossov University in Moscow.

"Good afternoon, my name is Sergei Abrossimov." He launched immediately into a lengthy monologue, exposing the major problems in the GDR, among them shortages of food, fuel, and consumer goods. Then he closed with the words: "The situation in the GDR is concerning. We cannot allow further unrest in our bloc. If the economic situation deteriorates any more, the people might lose faith in the socialist system. Thus, we must act swiftly and decisively."

"I wholeheartedly agree." Norbert pulled out the sheet of paper he'd prepared to present the measures the government had already taken. "We have increased production quotas, raised farmers' taxes, disallowed any and all private business, and..." His lips curled upward thinking of Rosalie's brilliant suggestion, "...we have set measures in motion to stop the drain of qualified workers."

Semjonov nodded. "That is laudable." Then he waved at Abrossimov, who walked up to the blackboard and picked up a piece of chalk.

Norbert sighed inwardly, he hadn't come here to be schooled by some lad half his age, who wouldn't last six weeks in real life with his theoretic approach. Alas, there was nothing he could do but to grin and bear it.

"With all due respect, Comrade Gentner, concrete actions are needed to prevent your country's collapse and thus potentially triggering a spark of revolt across the entire Eastern bloc, creating more devastation than the war did."

"I see." Norbert gave a sour smile, feeling as if he'd just been blamed for the problems of the entire Socialist world.

"We have prepared a catalog of measures for the recovery of the political situation in the GDR. First of all, you need to ease your citizens' economic burden. Your government has set unrealistic production quotas that are impossible to meet."

"They aren't. We have calculated—"

Semyonov, who was technically superior to the GDR government, raised a hand. "Listen first, complain later, comrade."

Abrossimov continued: "Your population is frustrated and angry. You have failed to ensure fair distribution of goods and resources."

Norbert exchanged glances with Rosalie, who was as aghast at the accusations as he was. What did this baby-faced, newly-graduated economist know about the real world? Ruling a country wasn't akin to pushing around numbers on a blackboard.

"Here's my plan. We'll call it the *New Course* and sell it to the population as the sole way to swiftly turn the situation around. It involves a bit of self-criticism, though." For the first time Abrossimov smiled.

"I know everything about Comrade Khrushchev's New Course," Norbert said curtly. "I think it's a brilliant move concerning Soviet foreign policy, and will surely relax the strained relations with the warmongering West by promoting détente; it is less useful for solving economic problems."

"You'll soon find out how useful it actually is. First, you'll dial back on the raising of the production quota, thus assuring that growth won't be reached by breaking your workers' backs." Abrossimov chalked several tables on the blackboard.

"Lowering the quota will prove detrimental to economic growth." Norbert had discussed this with the cabinet. The much-touted New Course was prone to weakening the Soviet system and was, in essence, a capitulation to the West. Therefore, they had decided to forge their own path, pushing collectivization forward, which meant increased state control over agriculture, construction, and the other sectors of the economy.

"It won't. You'll see. My team has done the calculations. Lower quotas, combined with bonus payments for extra achievement, will heighten individual motivation and thus production. Anyway, this isn't the only measure. We have further identified the treatment, Junge Gemeinde members receive, as a main driver of the population's discontent.

"The Junge Gemeinde is a terrorist organization, conspiring with the Imperialist west and undermining our very core values. This has forced us to implement harsh measures against their members: students will be expelled from school, or thrown into prison. Promoting their ideas is forbidden, hefty fines are issued for anyone caught with leaflets or similar illegal promotional material."

"Exactly," Semyonov said. "Under any other circumstances, I would approve of such measures, but in the current situation this might be the straw that breaks the camel's back. I suggest you rescind all regulations against members of the Junge Gemeinde and let them return to their schools or universities."

A barely audible gasp came from Rosalie, while Norbert's eyes widened. This foolish suggestion was political suicide. Rescind measures? Admit failure? How on earth would this help to prevent a catastrophe?

"It may sound counterintuitive, but our research has proven it's the only way to go forward. People seem to object to the infringement on their constitutional right of religious freedom." Semyonov's deep voice filled the room, leaving no doubt who had the final say here.

"With all due respect, Comrade Semyonov, you know as well as I do that those rights exist only on paper." Norbert desperately tried to defend his way of ruling the country.

A benevolent smirk pursed the old man's lips. "You and I may be aware of this, but the general public is not. In the current situation it's our fundamental task to prevent further unrest. Once the situation has stabilized you can tighten the thumb screws once more."

"If you are certain this is the solution, I will naturally implement your suggestions." Norbert was aware that none of the things mentioned were mere suggestions—they were definite orders.

"Another point is the press." Abrossimov chalked another picture depicting the media landscape in the GDR. "According to our analysis, the state-controlled media is not doing enough to disseminate positive messages about the government policies to counter the false narrative of the Western press, which unfortunately many of your people seem to believe."

"This is indeed a constant grief. Every day we're seizing several tons of contraband Western printed material. What we cannot control is the radio; about three-quarters of our population live in areas near enough to West Germany to listen to capitalist radio stations."

"We're well aware of the technical inability to impede radio waves. Which is why you need to increase your propaganda efforts and suppress any dissenting voices."

This was easier said than done, since the East Germans were notoriously suspicious of everything that came from the government and, strangely, some of them preferred to believe the imperialist propaganda over their own leadership.

Rosalie spoke up. "My husband suggested to me that better antifascist border protection should be installed. It would be a bulwark against damaging influences from the West, but also discourage our own citizens from deserting their country, thus protecting not only us but all of our socialist brother countries, including the great Soviet Union."

Semyonov smiled. "Your husband is a very intelligent man. With our help, he'll soon beat the German nation back into shape."

Once again, Rosalie had saved his neck and turned the situation around. She truly was the best wife he could have wished for.

"Thank you for your vote of confidence, comrade." Norbert intended to use the praise to lessen the blow. "While I wholeheartedly agree with the necessities of your measures, it might be prudent to consider a more gradual approach to avoid escalating tension?"

Semyonov raised his hands, quietly fixing his gaze on Norbert for a few seconds before he said, "If you don't act swiftly, you might not have a nation in two weeks' time."

CHAPTER 13

F lori sat across the table from Vladi, her heart pounding with a mixture of excitement and apprehension. He was charming, intelligent, and handsome. His lazy smile made her stomach lurch and every accidental, or not-so-accidental touch, sent delicious tingles across her skin. Yet, there was an invisible barrier between them.

As much as she tried to resist his advances, she felt an undeniable pull toward this man who seemed so perfect in every way. Flori's emotions swirled within her, threatening to overpower reason. She had never experienced such a strong attraction to anyone before. Vladi was everything she had ever dreamed of, and yet she held herself back. She wondered if she had become too guarded, too afraid of anything that could disrupt the delicate balance of her life.

"How was your work day, Floriane?" Vladi always used her full name, making it sound special. His deep and velvety voice sent shivers down her spine, making her yearn to throw caution to the wind and give in to their mutual attraction.

"I crushed cocoa beans all day," she replied, somewhat embarrassed by her humble job.

"Hmm, I for one, love chocolate." His eyes lit up with desire as he leaned forward to whisper in her ear, "And that smell of chocolate on you? It makes me want to lick it off."

Blushing furiously, she backed away from him, despite the heat rushing through her veins. For a second, she allowed herself to dream about lying in his arms. Then reality reared its head; she could never take him home, since she and Katja shared the only bedroom in the apartment.

"Please be serious," she scolded him, feverishly trying to keep her aplomb. "It's a factory job, not exactly glamorous or desirable."

"It is very important to feed the population, though." Vladi's eyes locked with hers, and his expression became serious. "If you could choose any profession you wanted to, what would it be?"

The answer came faster than a bullet. "Fashion design. I love showcasing the beauty of a woman."

"You're the best advertisement of your talents."

Again, she flushed slightly. Before walking out with Vladi she had taken special care to make the most out of her limited wardrobe. Even Katja had noticed and commented on it.

"What keeps you from pursuing your dream?" He traced a finger down her cheek, leaving exhilarating trickles in its wake. She found herself leaning toward him, yearning for a kiss. His eyes shone with the same desire she felt, yet he did not kiss her, or even touch her eager lips with his finger. He was waiting for an answer.

It was a sweet and yet so irritating trait of his to always expect an answer to his questions, unlike most men who were content to talk about themselves and usually asked rhetorical questions.

Like an interrogator. She pushed the thought away; Vladi was a sales agent. Listening to his customers' wishes was what he did for a living.

"I was a sixteen-year-old orphan after the capitulation, with a ten-year-old sister to take care of. Working in a factory was the only job available for someone like me. I had to drop out of school years earlier due to the war."

"There's no reason to be ashamed of being a worker." Vladi

looked at her, the intensity of his gaze sending tingles of desire through her body. "You're doing your country a great service."

"If I were working in construction, maybe, but producing Vitalade and other chocolate substitutes?"

"In a socialist economy every worker is of equal value, despite each of us having different roles. You might not be able to carry a sack of cement, but you do something just as important." He took her hand, rubbing a thumb across the back of it. "These hard-working builders need proper food to maintain their strength. And they need little pleasures, such as the Vitalade you make, to keep their spirits up while they toil to reconstruct your country."

She was too swept up in his sweet words to ponder why he'd said 'your country' instead of 'our country'.

"I never thought about it that way."

"Socialism is morally superior to the capitalist system, where everyone is out for himself. Here, we are all equal, no matter if one is the prime minister or a pretty chocolate worker."

Flori had serious doubts about this theory, especially where the politicians were concerned. However, not wanting to ruin the mood, she returned to his question about her dream. "I've always had a knack for working with cloth. Since money has been so tight, and new furniture is but a fantasy, I have decorated our apartment with reused boxes, and patched together rags in different colors etc. to transform it into a cozy home."

"I'd love to see it." Again, his face hovered much too close to hers, his eyes full of sincerity and vulnerability. Another shiver raced down her spine: caused equally by excited anticipation of taking him home with her and dread at what he might think about the tiny, sparsely-furnished place.

He must have sensed her inner turmoil, because he surprised her by adding, "I'd love to, but it's too early for such a step. You are a very special person."

As the evening continued, Flori allowed herself to let go of her hesitation and fully enjoy Vladi's company. With each passing moment, his efforts to win her heart unraveled another layer of her caution, gradually replacing reservation with a blossoming love. All too soon, the night came to an end and Vladi took her home.

"It was a lovely evening, thank you," she said, as they arrived in front of her large-panel building.

"The pleasure was all mine. You're an extraordinary person." Vladi looked at her with so much restrained passion in his eyes, she couldn't resist going on her tiptoes to peck his cheek. The slight stubble tickled her skin, kindling her entire body aflame. With his hands heavy on her shoulders they seemed to stand there for an eternity, the unspoken question hanging in the air, mingling with the silent tension she felt.

"I should go now," she began hesitantly. "It's late and I have to get up early in the morning."

"Floriane," he murmured, his voice laden with emotion, as his hands wandered down her arms to enclose hers in a tender grasp. The way he pronounced her name sent shivers down her spine, melting her heart once more. "Will you allow me to properly kiss you? Please?"

She all but melted into a puddle at his feet. "I thought you'd never ask."

His delighted grin took her breath away and she pushed herself against him, the world around her ceasing to exist as his mouth met hers. Under the soft pressure she opened her lips. His probing tongue slipped inside, filling her mouth, evoking the most delicious sensations. Tingles of exhilaration shot down to her toes and up again, pooling deep down in her core.

Pressing closer against his broad chest, she felt every ripped muscle beneath, his body warmth, the soft pressure of his hands stroking her back, all while their kiss deepened.

She wished time would stop to preserve this moment forever. Unfortunately, the voices of passersby disturbed them and Vladi released her lips. Instantly, she felt the loss, wondering how on earth she'd fallen for this man so hard and so fast.

"I better leave, or you won't get any sleep tonight." Vladi was an example of restraint as he stepped back and took her hand to press a kiss on it.

His remark left her wanton and she wanted to plead: *Don't go.* Thankfully, she still possessed enough pride not to throw herself at him and beg to be taken right there and then.

"It was a wonderful evening, Vladi."

"May I see you tomorrow after work?" His throaty voice was a whispered promise.

"I'd love to." She waved at him one last time before climbing up the stairs to her apartment, the warmth of Vladi's kiss lingering on her lips.

She unlocked the door to find the lights out, and quickly disappeared into the bathroom. Several minutes later she slid into bed next to her sleeping sister. Listening to Katja's even breath she wished it was Vladi sharing her bed.

The next morning, she woke up before the alarm rang, having dreamt all night about Vladi's kiss. She looked at her sleeping sister and silently got up to ready herself for work. The poor mite was studying so hard until late at night, she should get another fifteen minutes of sleep.

When Katja didn't walk into the kitchen for breakfast, Flori returned to the bedroom to find her still sleeping.

"Get up, sleepyhead. It's time for school."

"Not going." Katja flipped the blanket over her head.

"Don't be silly, of course you're going." A horrible suspicion dawned on her. Last night she'd been too preoccupied to ask for the outcome of the criticism and self-criticism session.

"I'm not." Katja pulled away the cover, making a funny grimace. "I've been expelled from school."

"You...what?" The impact of her sister's words struck her so hard that she sunk to the edge of the mattress. "They can't just expel you when you have done nothing wrong."

"It seems you're pretty alone with your opinion." Katja scrunched up her nose. "They accused me of every crime under the sun until I couldn't take it any longer and told them to stuff their bigotry where the sun doesn't shine."

"Katja!"

"It's true. Socialism might be wonderful in theory; what these people do is despotism, pure and simple. They say one thing, while doing the other. Making sets of rules for the population and a separate one for themselves. I'm sick and tired of the lying, the bigotry, the oppression, the spying, the denouncing, the kowtowing…I'm done."

"Katja!" Flori had no idea how to respond. Her academic little sister, the A-student on track to study engineering, had turned into a rebel. "Have you been approached by imperialist spies?"

"What?"

"Or where did you get these damaging ideas from?"

"I got them by using my brain. If you'd care to pause and think for a minute, you'd find out for yourself. The whole imperialist influence is a big, fat lie. It's one more thing they keep saying to keep us oppressed."

For a long time, Flori had been feeling inferior to her clever sister. It was true: after toiling for ten or more hours at the chocolate factory, she never found the time or energy to challenge political and economic wisdom propagated by the media. The whole misery of it suddenly burst out.

"And this is my fault? I have to put food on the table for both of us. Do you think I love my job? Do you think I happily break my back every day without being appreciated? Do you know why I'm doing all of this?"

Katja's face was a bewildered mask.

"For you! So you can graduate and go to university. So you can pursue your dreams and live the life you want to. I'm doing all of this for you, and now you tell me you destroyed your chances, and packed it all in, because you were too proud to grovel during the self-criticism session?"

The fight seeped out of her. Her hands in her lap, she closed her eyes, because she didn't want Katja to see her tears.

"I'm sorry." Katja put her hand on Flori's shoulder. "It's just... everyone keeps telling me how bad the Nazis were and how we have to fight fascism every step of the way, but nobody seems to recognize that what Stalin did, what our government now does, is exactly the same. Fascism disguised as socialism."

Flori gasped loudly. "You can't say that. If someone reports you to the Stasi..."

"You're not going to turn me in, are you?"

"Of course not. But it's better to be careful, you know how thin these walls are."

"And that's the reason why I want to leave." Katja sat up in bed, looking suddenly very mature.

"Oh sweetie, I know you want to live on your own, it's a step every young woman has to take at some point in her life." Flori felt a weight pressing down on her chest. She'd taken care of Katja for such a long time, she couldn't imagine ever being without her. It must be the way a mother might feel when her children spread their wings.

"That's not what I meant." Katja's face grew serious. "I want to leave the GDR, enjoy freedom in the West."

Flori swallowed down the lump forming in her throat. *"Republikflucht* is illegal. We have to stay here and make the best of it."

"Have you ever wondered why they made it illegal to leave our country?"

"Because..." Flori paused to ponder the question, for none of the explanations she'd heard actually made sense. Usually, the government explained the border controls were needed to protect the young republic from bad outside influences. Or to restrict currency flowing out, thus causing major economic rifts.

She shrugged.

"See? There's no valid reason, except for their hunger for power. We are their slaves and they can't let us go, or their entire system would crumble." Katja's voice was triumphant.

"Now you're exaggerating." Flori's heart constricted. Whether her sister's assessment was true or not, she didn't care. She didn't want to leave her hometown, her modest comfort, her friends, the familiar surroundings. Yes, she preferred the known circumstances to an unknown future somewhere in West Germany, alone in a capitalist country where everyone was out to get you. And…she didn't want to leave Vladi behind.

"I'm not and you know it. Sooner or later I'll leave this place and I'd love to take you with me."

"I'm much too old for a fresh start." Flori put her hands up in protest.

Katja guffawed. "You just turned twenty-four that can hardly be considered elderly." Her sister was right, yet Flori often felt like an old woman.

"I need to get going or I'll be late for work." She kissed Katja on the cheek. "We'll chat this evening."

CHAPTER 14

East Berlin, Early June 1953

Heated arguments flew back and forth across the room. Max grabbed the water jug on the table, poured himself a glass and downed it in one gulp.

"The workers are the backbone of our economy, but the government won't listen to us."

"Raised quotas or increased work hours is their only answer. As if it were our fault that the construction industry is behind schedule, when the actual reason is we're lacking raw material, heavy machinery and whatnot."

"We're not going to break our backs for the ruling class anymore. This is not socialism! We have the same rights as those ministerial lackeys."

"The SED must ease the conditions, or we'll all die from exhaustion."

"They will never agree to ease up," shouted Wagner from the Builders Union.

"How is it possible that workers are facing economic hardships in spite of toiling harder than ever before and attaining higher production targets?"

"Everyone in the country suffers from shortages of essential goods, high prices, and poor living conditions. Something has to give."

"My men are almost out of control. Every day is a struggle to keep them from rioting." Schultz, representing the Saxonia builders, was literally pulling his hair out.

"Right. We need improved working conditions, especially better security. And higher wages."

Max had been listening intently. Now he sensed the time had come to make a bold suggestion. He cleared his throat.

"All of you are right, and you know it. Our productivity targets are unattainable. We don't have proper equipment. Deadlines are putting extra pressure on my builders. And the government doesn't seem to take our grievances seriously." He paused, eyeing each one of his union leader colleagues, before he said, "We must strike."

In the ensuing commotion, he couldn't understand a single word. Realizing just how bold his suggestion was, he opted to give them some time to consider it. After all, in the Soviet Union, to whom the SED looked for guidance in everything they did, workers never went on strike.

The – ridiculous – explanation was that the people were the state and thus would effectively strike against themselves, harming the very people they wanted to help. He'd never bought into the ideological garbage that came with socialism.

"We've already seen small protests and skirmishes," Max said.

"Sure, but the authorities always shut them down quickly."

"Because they were isolated. If we organize a coordinated action across the country, they won't be able to do so."

"That's an interesting idea." Schultz rubbed his chin, whereas Wagner shook his head. "A strike will only damage ourselves."

"You don't really believe that garbage, do you?" Max fixed his gaze on the older bull-necked man, who'd worked in construction all his life.

"I keep my head low. Haven't made it through two World Wars and Hitler's fascist reign by protesting," Wagner grumbled.

"We're living in a democratic republic though," Schultz chimed in. "This isn't a terror regime mowing down its own workers and farmers."

Max fervently hoped Schultz was right. He'd suggested the strike despite a queasy feeling in his gut. The SED and their Soviet overlords weren't exactly known to use kid-gloves on dissidents.

"For all I care, if you think it'll help, I'm with you." Wagner clapped his hands. "When and where?"

Max pulled out a huge piece of paper, and unrolled it onto the table for them to write down the details. Late at night, he returned home, where Katja was waiting for him, half asleep, crouched in front of his door.

"What's up?" He held out his hand to help her up.

"Flori and I had a row. Can I stay with you tonight?"

"Absolutely not." The thought of her sleeping over shot heat into his groin, making him doubt his own ability to treat her with the respect she deserved. After their first kiss, he'd constantly thought about how magnificent it would be to make love to her. He shook his head to remind himself that this wasn't about to happen anytime soon. He loved her way too much to rush things and possibly frighten her away.

"Why not? Don't you like me anymore?" She pressed her lips against his, taking his breath away. Despite his heart hammering like thunder against his ribs, he somehow managed to free himself from her embrace.

"I like you far too much." His guilty grin must have betrayed his raging desire, because her eyes widened.

"Can I at least come in for a hot chocolate?"

Hearing steps behind his neighbor's door, he nodded. "Better not wake anyone up. Come in."

Max had just locked up behind them when he heard the nosy neighbor, who lived opposite him, opening his door to peek out, no doubt chasing some juicy gossip.

"Did you have to work this late?" Katja asked while she followed him into the kitchen.

"We had a union meeting. It was rather agitated." Max boiled water, for lack of milk. Then he took the Vitalade powder from the shelf and stirred it in. "What about you and Flori?"

"She's furious with me for being expelled from school."

"And rightly so. What possessed you to respond in the way you did? I'm surprised you got off so lightly." He handed her a mug filled with the steaming liquid.

"Lightly? They kicked me out for speaking the truth. What kind of system is that?" The rebellious glimmer in her eyes made her even more attractive, but he couldn't admit to it. For her own good he had to be stern with her.

"It's our system. You should have known better. Less than two months left in school and you got yourself expelled...for what?"

"For the truth." She stubbornly pressed her lips together.

"Don't you remember the old saying 'Loose lips sink ships'? It's important to know when to speak out and when to keep your mouth shut." He reflected on the meeting with the union leaders. Their time to speak out had definitely come.

Katja groaned, put the empty mug on the table and flopped on the sofa. "I've been looking for work."

"How did it go?" He raised an eyebrow. There weren't many jobs for high school dropouts without any vocational training – or with the stigma of being considered politically unreliable.

"Tough." Her expression clearly indicated that she didn't want to go into detail, so Max resisted commenting on it. "I thought I might work with your company."

"As a builder?" Max guffawed. "You do know that my workers regularly lug around sacks of cement?"

"I could do that." Her eyes narrowed with defiance.

"No doubt, once or twice, but not eight hours straight. That's men's work. Anyway, I'm not the one assigning the jobs. You'd have to go to the labor office."

"I went there," she mumbled. "Those imbeciles told me to finish high school first."

A wave of sympathy hit him, realizing how Katja was caught in a quandary with no obvious solution. "That doesn't leave you many options, now does it?"

She cocked her head, scrutinizing his face. "I'm going to join the protests."

"What protests?" Instantly he was on high alert, his entire being wanting to keep her out of harm's way.

"Oh, come on, don't tell me the unions don't know about them. Workers have taken to the streets to protest our miserable living conditions." She gazed at him, suspicion entering her eyes. "Of course you know about them. That was what your union meeting was all about, to suppress the protesters."

"On the contrary, we planned a coordinated strike to show the government we're serious." The moment the words left his mouth he regretted them. Now there was no way to keep Katja from pestering him until she'd wormed out every last detail from him. In a preemptive defense, he ordered, "You're not going to join."

She raised her chin, a spark of defiance entering her eyes. "Watch me walking the picket line!"

"Please Katja, this is no game," he pleaded, settling on the sofa next to her. "Promise you won't join the protests, it's dangerous."

"So why do you participate?" she asked, snuggling into his embrace. Warmth spread through his body.

"Who says I do?" His hand rubbed up and down her back.

"The union is organizing a strike and you're going to sit in your office watching from the sidelines? I don't think so."

Max groaned. This woman knew him too well. Their love relationship was so fresh, he tended to forget that they'd known each other almost all their lives.

"I'll be there in an official mode, they can't arrest me. Even if they do, they'll have to let me go. You, on the other hand…you have no reason to be there."

"Except to demonstrate for freedom and justice. Isn't that reason enough?"

"Not in the eyes of our government." He leaned his head against the backrest, pondering what he'd just said. He'd basically declared moral bankruptcy of the GDR regime. "Perhaps you were right after all," he murmured softly to himself.

"I'm tired." She slipped out of her shoes, putting her feet on the sofa.

"Then I better take you home. We don't want Flori to worry about your whereabouts."

"Spoilsport," she protested, but didn't put up any resistance when he helped her up and accompanied her to the next tower in the same building block.

"Goodnight sweetheart." He gave her a sweet kiss before returning home, both worried and giddy with anticipation about the planned strike.

One thing was sure: things would change. There simply was no way to predict the outcome.

CHAPTER 15

June 12, 1953

Vladi was looking forward to the weekend, which he intended to spend with Flori. He hadn't been able to see her all week, because after Norbert's return from Moscow, the entire GDR government, including Vladi, had spent day and night working out the best wording to inform the general public about the new course. On June 11th, the SED mouthpiece *Neues Deutschland* had printed an article with the title 'Communique of the Politburo of the Central Committee of the SED' on the first page, announcing the New Course.

"That should ease the tensions," Vladi said to Rosalie, as she served him real coffee, a luxury not many people in the GDR had the opportunity to buy.

"Norbert thinks it's too radical and we should have spread out the implementation of all these measures over several weeks." She sat on the chair opposite him, in their beautiful home in a sealed-off villa neighborhood in Pankow. The area was located next to the Schönhausen Palace, official residence of President Wilhelm Pieck. The general public was kept out by a board fence, and the only entrance was strictly guarded. No one came in here unannounced.

"If Abrassimov thinks this is the way to go, I would trust him; he's a gifted analyst." The young man was much too staid for Vladi's liking, lacking any sense of humor – but he didn't have to like the man to appreciate his keen mind.

"We'll see." Rosalie cast him a pleasant smile just before the door opened and Norbert strode inside, a deep frown creasing his forehead.

Vladi observed his hunched shoulders, the tired gait, the balding head. Norbert was not only getting old, approaching sixty, but also looked worried. Might he be haunted by the thought of losing his iron grip on his nation?

Norbert's often repeated motto was: "Whatever we do must look democratic, but we must control everything."

It was one of the reasons Moscow loved him so much. His strict control of the population, combined with absolute obedience to whatever the Kremlin wanted him to implement. Although, in recent months, he'd taken things a bit too far in his attempt to be the model socialist student.

The New Course attempted to ease back on some of the harsher measures, giving the illusion of political freedom to the workers and farmers. Despite having been indoctrinated right from the cradle, Vladi realized that a man under socialism did not have freedom. He consoled himself with the knowledge that it was a necessary evil during the transition from an inhumane capitalist society to the final state of a fair socialist society where everyone blossomed. It was a future he yearned for, hoping it wouldn't be too long in the making.

"It was a mistake. Give them an inch and they will take a mile." Norbert slapped a bunch of papers with the news of skirmishes around the country onto the table. "We promised leniency with religion and to end the quarrel with the church, to review prison sentences including the release of prisoners, and the return of property to peasant families and tradesmen. We have rescinded tax and price increases. We even prioritized the production of food and consumer goods over the heavy industries. And what do those louts do?"

"Clamor for more?" Rosalie looked at her husband, love shining in her eyes.

Vladi had never reconciled the two personalities of this woman: a loving, devoted, kind older lady in private, intelligent, humorous and a perfect host, versus one who didn't hesitate to push the hardest punishment onto her people.

"The construction workers want to go on strike."

"Don't they know this will only hurt themselves?" Vladi asked.

"I believe they do. Individual greed is what keeps them going, that and malicious influence from the West, where workers strike all the time." Rosalie turned toward her husband, "You're not going to give in to that, are you? After all the concessions the SED has already announced, it would be seen as a declaration of political bankruptcy."

"Moscow has put me in a predicament with their New Course." Norbert seemed to remember that Vladi was a representative of the Kremlin and turned in his direction, explaining, "You know how much I value Semjonov and his advice, but he doesn't know the German psyche as well as I do. Easing in the concessions would have been preferable to the swift move we made."

"I am not well-enough versed on the matter to be able to judge the implications." Vladi considered Norbert and Rosalie his friends, yet he would never utter a critical word that might end up with him sitting between them and the Kremlin.

Vladi's neck hair stood on end under Norbert's stare and he had to remind himself that he was the boss here, not the other way round. He'd been sent by General Propov to make sure the German nation stayed on track with the socialist ideology.

"Perhaps it is time to show some strength?" Rosalie suggested with a pleasant smile.

"We need to get an overview of the situation first," Norbert added. After a barely perceptible wink from him, his wife spoke again. "We need to get feet on the ground to ascertain the public opinion. Someone skilled in subtle interrogation while at the same time seamlessly blending in with the protesters."

Vladi had known the Gentners long enough to know what Rosalie was doing. He inwardly shrugged nonchalantly at the idea of her believing she'd manipulated him into agreeing to her scheme. Since it was aligned with the task Beria had given him, he'd gladly play her game. To tell the truth, he was exhilarated at the possibility of getting involved in some riots – it would provide the excitement he lacked in his rather comfortable existence.

"Neither of us can do it, since we're much too well-known. We'll have to send in a request to the Stasi," Norbert said, rubbing his chin.

"You know how slow they can be, especially now they're so busy arresting rioters." Rosalie moved her head back and forth as if thinking hard, forcing Vladi to cough to disguise his chuckle. It was a spectacular show the two of them were giving, but oh so easy to see through.

"Time really is a constraining factor. Don't you have a suitable man at your disposal, perhaps one of your bodyguards?" Vladi said to keep up the charade.

"We'd have to do some moving around…" Norbert mused, and then Rosalie interrupted, delivering the final attack, "I was thinking…dearest Vladi…if it wouldn't inconvenience you too much? We'd be so grateful for your help."

"Me?" He feigned surprise. "I wouldn't even know where to go."

"I'll arrange everything for you. We'll supply a car with a driver and radio telephone." In a clear sign this had been planned out in advance, she casually pulled a map from a drawer and pointed out the route southward to Halle and Leipzig. "We'll organize a room in the best hotel in Leipzig for you. If you stay overnight it'll give you the opportunity to continue to Chemnitz, Dresden and Cottbus the next day, before returning to Berlin. What do you say?"

"I'm happy to help, I'll just have to inform General Propov. May I use your telephone?"

"Be my guest."

After advising his superior of the plan he returned to the living room, half expecting Rosalie to be waiting with his fully packed suitcase, ready to usher him out of her home.

111

"Since speed is of great importance I was thinking we could ask the maid at your residence to pack a suitcase for you and have it delivered to the hotel tonight. Would that be convenient for you?" she asked, putting her hand on his arm in a motherly way."

"I have everything I need." Vladi smiled innocently at her, not letting Rosalie see that he knew the whole plan was preconceived. He merely wondered if there was also a hidden reason why they wanted to get him out of Berlin so quickly.

He arrived in a town near Leipzig and made his way through the bustling streets, suddenly captivated by a raucous commotion up ahead. Curiosity piqued, he quickened his pace, eager to understand the cause of the gathering crowd. As he drew nearer, the scene unfolded before his eyes in a shocking display of civic unrest.

A group of impassioned impromptu protesters had taken matters into their own hands, their fervent voices echoing through the air.

"Go home!" the mayor ordered over his loudspeaker. "Protests are illegal. Go home and wait for the government to consider your grievances."

His attempt to placate didn't sit well with the rioters. Dissatisfaction was visible on the grim faces of most every man or woman on the street. Vladi joined the crowd, keeping in the background. The heated atmosphere stirred the masses, similar to the enthusiasm he'd felt during the battle of Berlin in the Great Patriotic War. From experience he knew there was no way back once the boiling point had been reached, and he wondered what might happen next.

His question was resolved not much later, when a couple of strong-built men, fueled by righteous indignation, unceremoniously grabbed the mayor and dumped him into a nearby cesspit. Vladi gasped into the general outcry. The shock of such a blatant disregard of the authorities left him reeling, his eyes wide with disbelief at the boldness of the scene that unfolded before him.

Seconds later, bystanders, perhaps disapproving of the extreme action, rushed to the mayor's aid. With a collective effort, they managed to pull the distressed man out of the filth-ridden abyss. As soon as he was on firm ground again, the mayor blustered at the masses, promising severe punishment, which nobody seemed to take seriously. Vladi had seen enough. He disappeared into an alley, making a beeline for his car.

"We better leave this place, before it gets any more unpleasant," he told the driver. "Please radio Herr Gentner's office to send police. The rioters are so heated they will stop at nothing to vent their anger and people will be harmed if the revolt isn't quelled."

"Certainly, Colonel Rublev," Axel said.

For the rest of the day, Vladi witnessed many more skirmishes. Fortunately, nothing as egregious as a government representative thrown into a cesspit. In the evening, a glass of vodka next to him, he poured his observations into his field report, urgency driving each keystroke as he relayed vital information to the GDR government, the SSC and General Propov.

East Germany resembled a powder keg, ready to explode with the smallest spark. If it blew up, it would take the entire Eastern bloc with it, encouraging countries like Czechoslovakia or Poland to follow their lead and rise up against their benefactor, the Soviet Union. This had to be prevented at all cost.

He closed the report destined for General Propov and Beria, by pointing out the threat of mayhem and recommending clandestine preparation to intervene if necessary. Then he leaned back, ordered a second vodka, and let his mind veer toward Floriane.

His heartbeat sped up as her beautiful face appeared before his inner eye, leaving him puzzled as to why he harbored such a profound affection for her. Never before had he formed, or wanted to form, a strong attachment. But with her, he almost understood his friend Grigori's decision to settle down.

CHAPTER 16

F riday afternoon and Flori looked forward to her last shift of the week ending soon. Vladi had promised they would spend the weekend together, making a trip to the lake Großer Müggelsee if the weather permitted, which, unfortunately, didn't look much like it, if today's showers didn't ease.

Nonetheless, she'd been giddy with anticipation ever since he mentioned the plan a few days ago. Not even the sorrow about Katja being expelled from school was able to wipe the smile from her face as she imagined the day with Vladi by her side.

"Dreaming about that handsome chap again?" Klara asked, as she lugged another sack of raw materials to the grinding station.

"Is it so obvious?" Flori giggled.

"He truly is a looker and seems to be quite important. I saw him last night stepping out of a government car."

"Are you sure it was him?" Flori scrunched up her nose. Vladi had never mentioned any government business.

"Very sure. I stopped to take a second look, because he was wearing a uniform."

"Uniform? That's impossible. What kind of uniform?"

"Soviet."

Flori shook her head. "You must be mistaken, he's not a Russian."

Klara shrugged. "Maybe you're the one who's mistaken?"

Anger bubbled up in Flori, but she couldn't reply because, at that very moment, the foreman passed their station. She and Klara quickly resumed their work, neither wanting to be reprimanded for idle chitchat.

Klara was an incorrigible gossip, who'd seen Vladi once in a bar. Surely, she must have mistaken him for someone else. There was no reason Flori should believe her, yet a doubt remained. Sighing, she decided to confront him when he came to pick her up this evening.

She arrived home to find Katja waiting with dinner, beaming from ear to ear.

"What's up with you? Did you win the lottery?" Flori asked, slipping out of her drenched shoes and putting the umbrella into the bathtub to dry.

"Almost. You'll never guess!" Katja jumped up and down like a little girl.

"Hmm. Max asked you out on a date?"

"Yes." If possible, Katja's face beamed brighter. "But that's not the reason. Guess again."

Flori was too exhausted after the hard week to rack her brain. Raising her hands in defeat, she said, "I don't have the slightest idea."

"The school sent a message that I'm allowed to return come Monday and will be admitted to the graduation exams. Isn't that great news!"

"That's brilliant. I'm so happy for you." Flori hugged her little sister, and together they danced through the living room. "How come they changed their mind?"

"Haven't you read the SED's communique? All Christian students have to be readmitted to school."

"But you're not Christian, you were expelled for insubordinate conduct." Flori tugged a strand of hair behind her ear.

"It seems, because I was doing it to defend Liese, who is now reinstated, they gave me the same second chance, in exchange for my undying gratitude to the socialist system." Katja's tone was so full of mockery, Flori involuntarily flinched.

"Please watch your tongue, at least until after your graduation, they certainly won't give you a third chance."

"Don't worry. Outside these four walls I'll be the perfect example of an obedient, devoted, socialist citizen. No word of criticism will leave my lips." Katja put her fingers to her mouth, pretending to turn a lock.

Flori giggled. "Now that would be nice for a change."

The doorbell rang and she hurried to get it.

"Waiting for your suitor?" Katja teased, as she raced her sister to the door. They both reached for the knob at the same time and hauled the door open, to find a messenger outside, looking slightly confused.

"Floriane Eilers?" he asked.

"That's me."

"I have a message for you." He handed her a plain brown envelope and disappeared down the stairs.

"Who is it from?" Katja, as usual, poked her nose into everything.

"I don't know." Flori flipped over the envelope printed with her name and address, but didn't find a sender on the back.

"Open it." Katja seemed even more curious than her sister.

"Give me some space, will you?" Flori walked into the kitchen to open the letter with a knife and unfolded a piece of paper to find a scribbled note.

Dearest Florian,

I'm so sorry, business has required me to travel out of town and I won't be back until Sunday afternoon. Please accept my apologies for ruining our weekend plans. I promise to make it up to you.

Missing you dearly,
Vladi.

. . .

Staring with unbelieving eyes, she wanted to cry with disappointment.

"Well, what did it say?" Katja had followed her into the kitchen.

"Nothing." Flori tried to gather her composure. This wasn't the end of the world. "My suitor, as you like to call him, had to travel out of town and cancelled our weekend plans."

"I'm sorry. If you want, you can join Max and me…"

"No thanks. I have no desire to be the third wheel, watching you love birds whisper sweet nothings." Flori swallowed down the lump forming in her throat, as Klara's earlier remark sprung to mind. Was Vladi leading a double life? How much did she actually know about him? But then, if he wanted to hide something, he surely wouldn't send her a messenger, now would he?"

Another ring of the doorbell indicated a second visitor. This time Flori didn't bother to get it. Staying in the kitchen she heard Max's voice, then nothing for quite a while, and finally some heavy puffing.

Soon afterward, when her sister returned to the kitchen, her face was flushed with heat. A pang of jealousy stabbed her heart.

"Max is having dinner with us before we go out," Katja announced, her voice so happy that Flori immediately forgot her envy. She didn't begrudge her sister the happiness with Max, she simply wanted the same for herself with Vladi.

Over dinner, the conversation inevitably turned toward the announcement of the government's New Course.

"I hope this will change things for the better," Flori said. She so much wanted to believe in a brighter future, although life experience warned her to be skeptical.

"Only time will tell. For now, the protests have sped up." Max always knew more than the rest, due to his high position in the union.

"Why would people protest about the New Course? Isn't it what everyone was clamoring for?" Flori took another forkful of pasta with tiny bits of ham sprinkled through.

"It's complicated. Some people say it's an admission of political failure and want to overthrow the government."

Flori held back a gasp. Despite all the shortcomings of the socialist ideology, it was a lot better than Hitler's reign of terror. She certainly had no desire to go back to the utter chaos and destruction of the days leading up to the capitulation – nor to the legal vacuum during the immediate aftermath.

"The main issue though, is that the increase in labor standards remains in place. This has fueled the discontent among the builders. I'm sure the workers at your factory aren't pleased, either." Max tucked into his meal as if he hadn't eaten for days. Yet another reminder of how much better life had become under the SED. People might moan and groan about not being able to buy real chocolate, but at least no one had to go to bed on an empty stomach, the way Flori had been forced to do in the last throes of the war and beyond.

"No, we are certainly not happy with the new targets." Flori frowned. "We're breaking our backs as it is, and the authorities are immune to our complaints."

"If they were rational, they would look into the unrest among workers," Max exclaimed, waving his fork in the air as he worked himself up into a rage. "But no, those responsible engage in nothing but futile games! I was at the construction site preparing for the new project when three government representatives arrived, wanting to discuss increases in standards. How about they increase our wages for once?"

"Enough of politics, I'm getting a headache," Katja retorted.

"That's the new Katja, she's gone over to the dark side." Flori grimaced. "She's become a party-line-toeing communist!"

"I am nothing of the sort!" Katja protested vehemently. "Weren't you the one who told me never to utter a word of criticism ever again?"

Flori sighed. "I did. You've just been reinstated at school and will soon attend university, a first in our family. We may not agree with everything the SED does, but it speaks well for the country that an orphaned child without financial means can become an engineer. We should give the government the benefit of the doubt; in due time things will change, you'll see."

"I hope they will, however I won't bet my salary on it." Max served himself seconds, asking if the girls wanted more too, before he emptied the bowl onto his plate. Mopping up the last bit of sauce with a piece of bread, he complimented them, saying, "That was one of the best meals I've ever had."

"Katja cooked it all on her own." Flori was proud of her little sister.

"She's grown up, hasn't she?" Max's eyes shone with love and Flori couldn't have wished for a better man for her sister. He'd certainly make a good husband and father when the time came.

"We better get going, if we want to be punctual," Katja said, grabbing the plates to clear the table.

"I'll do it. You go and have fun tonight." Flori hugged first her sister and then Max, whispering into his ear, "Take good care of her, won't you?"

"Always." He grinned like a lovesick fool.

CHAPTER 17

Max held Katja's hand as they descended the stairs, their fingers intertwined. Stepping onto the street, his heart hammered against his ribs. It was the first time they'd publicly shown their deep affection for each other, and he couldn't be happier.

"I have loved you for a long time, Katja." Max's expression grew serious, his voice filled with heartfelt sincerity and emotion. "I want you to know that I am wholeheartedly committed to you."

Without a moment's hesitation, Katja responded, "I feel the same way. I have loved you forever, Max. What took you so long to tell me?"

"I was waiting for you to grow up," he replied, caressing her cheek gently. Dark thoughts formed in his mind and he squeezed her hand hard. "Whatever anyone tells you, please know that I would rather die than hurt you."

She stopped in her tracks, turning to scrutinize him, her eyes sparkling with love – and worry. "Are you in trouble, Max?"

"No." He looked around to see whether anyone was within earshot. "It's just… I have a bad feeling."

"About what?"

"There's so much discontent among the workers. I've been

constantly talking with the bosses and the government to voice our concern, but they simply won't listen."

Katja broke out into her wonderful sparkly giggle. "That's absolutely normal. They never do. You've been complaining about it for years. Why would you suddenly be so concerned about their refusal to collaborate instead of dumping nonsensical orders onto your heads?"

"This time it's different. You have no idea how explosive the atmosphere is. Even hard-core socialists are enraged. The New Course is nothing but a slap in the face."

"How so?" Katja raised an eyebrow. "Isn't it a good thing they are loosening the restrictions? I wouldn't be back at school if not for the New Course."

"It's not that simple. The government eased most of the restrictions, except for the increase in production quotas, claiming they were implemented on a voluntary basis, which couldn't be further from the truth. My men are livid. If the authorities don't concede soon, I fear for the worst." Max grimaced.

"What will they do?" She looked over her shoulder. "Flee to the West? And why would you be implicated?" Her face became fearful. "You're not going to flee, are you?"

He shook his head. "I still think our system is morally superior; it's just that the government abuses their power and turns socialism into something bad. I intend to stay and improve the conditions from within. Besides..." he cocked his head, "I would never leave without you."

Katja kept silent for a long time, biting her lower lip in thought. When she locked eyes with him again, her gaze was filled with steely determination. "I have learned a lot about our nation during the past weeks, and it's not been positive. Somehow, I don't believe our rulers will allow true change. The likes of Norbert Gentner will never give up the luxuries their positions provide."

"Be careful voicing these thoughts," Max warned her, his hand seeking hers again.

"I trust you and Flori with my life. She has raised me, often being more a mother than a sister. I love her to bits, you know, but I won't spend the rest of my life with her." Her eyes filled with so much love, Max's heart fluttered. "You're the one I want to spend my life with and, if you decide to flee, I'll come with you without a second thought."

Regardless of his emotion over her declaration of love, he warned, "This is not to be taken lightly. You can be imprisoned for leaving the country without permission, and it won't be nice."

Max shivered at the rumors he'd heard from the Stasi prison Hohenschönhausen, which was used mainly for political opponents, critics or dissidents. For obvious reasons, nobody talked openly about it, yet the grapevine whispered awful stories. After Stalin's death, the NKVD chief Beria had issued a ban on physical torture in all Socialist countries. According to an acquaintance who worked in Hohenschönhausen, the interrogators were now schooled in psychological torture instead.

"If you leave, I'll go with you. No discussion. I'm not a baby anymore," Katja insisted.

"As I said, I don't plan to escape, my work is cut out for me here. By the way, tomorrow some colleagues and I have an interview with the newspaper. Let's hope that'll bring some progress on the issue."

"I wish I could do more. For now, let's go to a corner bar for a beer."

"Now that's a plan!" Max grinned. There weren't many places to go in East Berlin, except for the corner bars with their air thick from cigarette smoke and bad music blaring from the radio.

It was late when he returned Katja to her apartment, before walking the short distance to his own place. The next morning, he rehearsed the issues he wanted to talk about with the journalist before meeting two colleagues in front of the Neues Deutschland headquarters, where the interview would take place.

"Thanks for agreeing to meet with me," greeted the journalist, Alice Berben.

"Thank you for taking an interest in the workers' issues," Max answered politely.

She led them to a small office, where she offered water and coffee before taking up paper and pencil. "As I said, your names won't be mentioned in the article, so you can speak frankly with me."

"We appreciate this." Max's coworker, Klaus Mattel, retrieved a bunch of notes from his briefcase. "We're not only speaking for ourselves, but for all comrades of the VEB Wohnungsbau, the residential construction kombinat."

"The entire nation is grateful for your commendable efforts to provide housing. Thus, it's alarming that some carpentry brigades in Stalinallee have refused to begin their work in the morning, claiming differences with the department setting the quota."

"Unfortunately, the discontent among many workers has been increasing. We all applaud the New Course and are eager to continue being *best-workers*, the way we have in the past. Yet, some of our comrades can't understand why so many regulations have been revoked, whereas the increase in production standards stays." Max didn't fully trust the journalist, so he made it sound as if he wasn't of the same opinion.

"One would think the management of our kombinat should address the discontent among the workers. But nothing of the sort has happened. Party representatives are not listening to our issues and certainly not taking measures to ease the conditions our comrades face," Klaus added.

"In fact, they have resorted to tricks and lies, even to outright blackmail to coax, for example, the bricklayer brigades into raising their standards." Max didn't mention the added threats, issued by the authorities, because of them supposedly being Western agents, all because the American radio sender RIAS had allegedly mentioned their refusal to increase workloads as evidence of the failed socialist experiment.

He still recoiled from this horrendous accusation, remembering how he'd felt as if they were putting a rope around his neck and pulling his legs away.

"If only someone had spoken to us directly, for once, I'm sure we would have raised our standards. We're not brutes, after all. But we're not going to have a gun put to our heads. And we're certainly not going to let the authorities play various parts of the brigade off against one another. We're comrades and we stick together." Klaus raised his fist in the air.

"Our payment is never correct. Every month we have to review the numbers and negotiate with the payroll department. Are we expected to beg for our wages as if we're asking for charity?" Max asked the journalist.

"Certainly not."

"You must understand us, Frau Berben, we want to work, we want to build. All of us want to bring our nation forward. We're proud citizens of the GDR, we're just very agitated because the authorities are not taking us seriously." Klaus was talking himself into a rage. "And not only the authorities! Our own standards department seems to have lost touch with us. These employees walk around in their business suits, looking down their noses at us, strutting through the construction sites while we are breaking our backs for the wellbeing of the country."

"So, you feel they are not on your side?" Frau Berben asked, as she jotted down a summary.

"We often get the feeling that the employees issuing the quotas want to make a good name for themselves, without any consideration for how it affects us. They seem to forget that without us construction workers, nothing will actually get done. The authorities should start recognizing that we are their allies and want to be treated as such." Max didn't resent these men's relatively easy job behind a desk. On the contrary, he was proud of the work he and his colleagues did. It irked him that these desk jockeys considered themselves to be above the workers, which was not only absurd, but also against the very ideology of the socialist workers' and farmers' state.

"What else do you want then?" Frau Berben chewed pensively on the back of her pencil.

"Not much." Max smiled at her. "Basically three points: first, there must be an end to horse-trading and standards-switching at will.

Secondly, a quota increase can be declared binding for a brigade only after the brigade members have agreed to the importance of this measure in our struggle for a better life for everyone. And third, the leading comrades in VEB Wohnungsbau must immediately desist with the whitewashing, the self-deception and arrogance. The party leadership needs to consider the builders in all their decisions and measures."

"That is a lot to ask," Frau Berben said.

Klaus shrugged. "The party leaders should work for a day on a construction site, humping chunks of concrete weighing a hundredweight! Let's see if they can still say to our faces afterwards, that our demands for construction hoists are unreasonable."

"Thank you for your constructive suggestions." Frau Berben finished the interview several minutes later.

"You won't print what we've told you in the newspaper, anyway." Max didn't hold any illusion that this journalist was going to endanger her career for a bunch of builders.

"Rest assured, I will." Her lips curled into a determined expression. "You're not the only ones discontented with some of the conditions in our state. Personally, I believe the thaw in relations after Stalin's death is the best chance we've ever had to implement true changes."

Then she accompanied them to the exit and bid them farewell. "Buy a newspaper tomorrow."

CHAPTER 18

Berlin, June 14th 1953

The phone rang. Vladi put the pillow over his head, refusing to wake up. He had returned to Berlin late last night and was planning to sleep at least until noon on this Sunday morning.

Alas, sleep was not in the stars for him. A persistent knock on his door was followed by the voice of his roommate, "Comrade Gentner on the phone for you."

Vladi peeked at the clock on his nightstand. It wasn't even eight in the morning, a fact that instantly rang alarm bells in his head. Neither of the Gentners were known to be early risers.

"What does he want? Can it wait?" Vladi tried to salvage what was left of his sleep.

"I'm sorry, but the comrade said it was urgent."

"Coming," Vladi grumbled, getting out of bed and walking toward the door of his room. As usual, he'd slept stark naked. He smirked, imagining the scandalized expression of his roommate if he strode into the living room in his current condition.

He had half a mind to do it just to unsettle the other man, but then thought better of it and slipped on a pair of underpants and a white, fine-ribbed singlet. He declined to put on a shirt, hoping the office-sitter would go green with envy when he saw Vladi's muscular frame.

As he'd expected, the other man's jaw dropped to the floor when Vladi passed him, flexing his abs just for the fun of it.

"Thank you for taking the call." Vladi grabbed the receiver, speaking into it. "Vladimir Rublev at your disposal. What can I do for you, Comrade Norbert?"

"Have you read the newspaper?" Norbert's voice sounded shrill.

"Not yet."

"It's catastrophic. Buy a copy and read the "wooden mallet" article on the way to my office. Emergency meeting in thirty minutes."

"Yes, comrade." Vladi was too stunned to remind Norbert that he wasn't supposed to give orders to a Soviet intelligence officer.

"Something up?" The officer-sitter had been waiting in the doorway, eavesdropping.

"Apparently a state crisis. I'm sure you'll be informed on a need-to-know basis." Vladi smirked. Back in his bedroom he eyed regretfully his black pants and leather jacket, before he put on his uniform. Twenty-eight minutes later he arrived at the government building and into a room full of functionaries.

As soon as he settled into a seat, an aide reported several protests following the publication of the so-called wooden-mallet article in the Neues Deutschland. In the already politically-charged climate, tensions ran high and the newspaper's article, shedding light on the workers' plight, seemed to have set fire to the tinder.

Across the country more and more demonstrations popped up, causing worry among the leaders. Vladi had experienced it firsthand during his trip to Leipzig and other towns; the people resented their leaders for the abuse of power, economic failures and poor planning. Regardless of the suppression of free speech by severe punishment, the atmosphere was full of a spirit of revolt.

It was most disconcerting.

"Who is responsible for this disastrous article?" Norbert yelled into the room.

"A journalist called Alice Berben."

"I want her in jail! Immediately! Order the Stasi to arrest and interrogate her. Threaten her with execution if she doesn't rescind her article!" Norbert was out of his mind. Nobody in the room dared to contradict him for fear of ending up in the same place he planned for Frau Berben.

Vladi bit his lip. He wasn't supposed to interfere with German government business. To be on the safe side, he should telephone General Propov and ask for instructions on how to deal with this mess. Although…Norbert behaving like a loose cannon and arresting a journalist, for a very moderate article, in this heated atmosphere might cause a greater uproar, ultimately endangering the Soviet hegemony in Eastern Europe.

No, Vladi couldn't bide his time. He had to keep this lunatic under control.

"Wouldn't that cause much greater trouble, arresting a journalist?" he asked into the room.

Instantly, all eyes were on him. Some surprised, others fearful, all of them secretly relieved that Vladi had spoken out loud what they all knew to be true. Only Norbert glared at him with anger.

"She's a traitor to the nation. She must be punished for her deeds," the most powerful man in the state insisted.

"Perhaps she must. But not right now." Vladi stood up, towering over the men seated at the long conference desk. "From what I've seen during the past days, the general public is eager to protest. You're losing control over your country and your first goal must be to get it back. Arresting this woman will further enrage the workers; it might be the spark lighting the tinder to burn your entire country to the ground. My superiors would not like that."

Norbert visibly swallowed. He knew that he owed his position, his power, his wealth, even his life exclusively to the support of the Soviet Union. Vladi might be his superior and friend, but Norbert was intelligent enough to recognize that a Russian officer served, above anything else, his country.

"If you insist." Norbert bowed his head. "What do you suggest we do instead?"

Suppressing a smirk, Vladi answered, "Reinforce the police in major cities, especially East Berlin. Quickly dissolve gatherings, before they transform into an organized protest. Call for a meeting with union leaders and ease their minds. Once the situation is under control, let's say in a few weeks from now, you can tighten the leash again."

Satisfied with his intervention, Vladi steepled his hands on the desk and kept silent for the remainder of the meeting. A couple of hours later, he took his leave. After a quick bite of lunch he decided to see whether Floriane was at home, fully intending to make up for the missed date on Friday night.

He found her at her apartment, together with Katja and a man who introduced himself as Max Hempel. Not showing his disappointment at the company, he greeted her with a chaste kiss on her cheek. "I hope I'm not interrupting anything."

"Not at all. I hadn't expected to see you so soon. Where have you been?"

"I was called away to an important business meeting in Leipzig." He furrowed his brow. "And then my boss used this as an excuse to have me visit several of our clients in the region."

"On a Saturday?" she asked, catching him unprepared.

He quickly regained his aplomb. "Those were the exact same words I used, but he insisted. Sometimes we need to go above and beyond to propel our country forward."

"Your country? Aren't you Russian?" Max asked in a slightly hostile tone.

"I'm not." Vladi positioned his feet hip-width apart, letting the other man know that he wasn't intimidated by his presence.

"Your name sure sounds Russian to me," Max insisted, narrowing his eyes.

"Max! Don't be so rude." Floriane rushed to Vladi's aid, stepping next to him.

"Don't be offended on my behalf. Your friend is right wanting to protect you from strangers." Vladi laced his voice with soft honey, a tone he'd practiced for years and which he knew women were powerless against. As he'd expected, Floriane bristled under the assumption that she needed protection.

"I'm old enough to take care of myself."

Vladi barely bit back a chuckle. Regardless of the unwelcome situation of having two more people in Flori's apartment, things were progressing according to plan and she'd soon be eating out of his hand. A week, or two at most, and she would passionately sink into his bed, where he'd take them both to the heights of incomparable pleasure.

He gently rubbed his thumb across the back of her hand; a gesture he knew conveyed trust. "My mother married a Russian. I never really got to know him, because he died when I was very young. After his death, mother and I returned to live with her family in Germany."

"Whereabouts?" Max wasn't satisfied with the answer. This didn't present a challenge, because Vladi had perfected his backstory over the years.

"We lived in Tilsit, a town which used to belong to Germany, but now is part of the Kaliningrad Oblast in the Soviet Union. My mother died during the war and I ended up in Berlin." To preempt further inquiries, Vladi added, "In theory, I could have returned to Tilsit, due to my Russian father, but I feel so much more connected with Germany." He put a hand over his heart, disarming Max with a nostalgic smile.

"Will you stop your inquisition now?" Floriane glared at Max, who gave a nod and a shrug. Vladi made a mental note to have a look into Max's Stasi file and keep an eye on him.

Much to Vladi's chagrin neither Katja nor Max made an attempt to excuse themselves, apparently determined not to leave Floriane alone with the man she so obviously was infatuated with.

Well, if he'd learned one thing in his intelligence career it was patience. A little more wining and dining, and Floriane was going to fall into his lap like a ripe fruit. Involuntarily, he licked his lips, savoring her delicious taste in his mind.

Two hours later he bid farewell, but not before asking Floriane for permission to pick her up from work on Tuesday.

CHAPTER 19

Tuesday, June 16th 1953

On her way to work, Flori passed the Stalinallee, where the biggest construction site in all of East Berlin lay. Each weekday, at seven a.m. sharp, thousands of workers of all trades took up their trowels, hammers, saws, or grinders, to build a better future.

Today though, the scaffoldings stood empty. No sound echoed through the air, making Flori check her wristwatch, thinking she'd accidentally left home early, but no, if anything, she was running late.

Even as she passed the street, turned a corner and descended to a side alley, where a smaller building was under construction, the same peculiar sight greeted her: empty sites. A strong sensation ran down her spine; a foreboding of momentous events to unfold.

She quickened her steps toward the chocolate factory, not wanting to be the target of Herr Schmidt's scorn in an atmosphere that was already reaching boiling point.

Wondering whether this was part of the strikes Max had insinuated might happen, she hastened into the locker room and changed into her uniform just in time to clock in as her shift began.

Stirring the mixture to make the chocolate substitute, Vitalade, she soon slipped out of reality to daydream about having a fashion design business. Instead of sweating in the sweltering factory hall, bent over boiling liquids, she'd sit at home, hunched over her sewing machine, making the most beautiful dresses from soft, silky cloth.

A smile tugged her lips. If only the government would allow her to leave her post at the factory and grant her a place at the *Institut für Bekleidungskultur*, the GDR's only institution to provide studies in fashion design.

Else, whose brother worked at the VEB Radio Television Technique, had proudly contributed the portable radio his company produced, to their department. Officially it was called Möwe 6D71, but due to the green plastic housing, the population had nicknamed it *Laubfrosch*, green frog.

Usually, the girls listened to music during their break, but today the ether was filled with news about the workers' strikes. It seemed that none of the construction brigades in East Berlin had gone to work this morning.

"I wondered why nobody was at the site in Stalinallee," Flori mused.

"When my husband told me about the planned strike, he made it sound as if it was just a few brigades," Carolin said.

"We should join them." Flori was surprised by her own boldness.

"We're not construction workers." Helga was always careful to toe the official party line.

"Who cares?" Klara put her hands akimbo. "If there's a protest, I'm going. There's so much we can do better in this country. It's about time we changed something!"

A stunned silence filled the room as the women glanced at each other, carefully hiding their shock at the bold words. Flori looked at each of her friends, seeing uncertainty, even fear in their eyes - except for Klara, who stood erect like a statue, her lower lip pushed out.

If her friend could protest, so could Flori. Weren't they supposed to stand together in a socialist society?

"I'll come with you," she finally said, glancing around at the stunned faces.

"One for all and all for one!" Else yelled into the breakroom, evoking fits of laughter. Her shout had broken the ice and, one by one, everyone in their department agreed to jointly march for more justice.

They weren't as courageous as the builders and decided to wait until their shift ended. Much too soon the lunch break was over and each dashed off to their respective workstation.

Throughout the afternoon, whenever colleagues from other departments dropped in on work errands, the strike was the topic of brief, heated disputes. A fresh breeze of optimism now replaced the former tense and depressed atmosphere.

"We've talked and begged. No one listened to our concerns. Now we must shape our own fortune," Klara rallied the newcomers. "We workers will make our voices heard!"

As their shift ended, exhilaration grabbed Flori. Together with her colleagues, she stepped out of the factory, marching toward the Stalinallee, where already several thousand people gathered. Someone carried a placard with the inscription *"Wir Bauarbeiter fordern Normsenkung"*, We construction workers demand a reduction in standards.

"Look at that." In awe, Flori nudged Klara.

"It's exhilarating, isn't it?" Klara hastened to join the crowd, dragging Flori and the others behind. When they almost reached the Stalinallee, another demonstration procession formed to march off along Leipziger Strasse to the seat of the government. Flori and the others followed, joining the chant.

"Colleagues, fall in line! We want to be free people!"

In front of the government building, the demonstrators demanded to speak to Grotewohl or Gentner, yet only subordinate officials showed up on the balcony. They were shouted down, running for the safety of the closed building again.

"The government is going to sit this out," Flori whispered.

"This time they won't get away with inertia. Have you seen how many people are here?" Klara turned around to take in the crowd which was still growing. Thousands upon thousands of Berliners were joining the protests.

"Don't you think we should leave?" Carolin resembled a frightened mouse.

"Leave now? Under no circumstances. We're here to change our future." Klara was on a roll, jumping, yelling, chanting.

Since neither Gentner nor Grotewohl showed up, a construction worker climbed the podium and called for a general strike for tomorrow.

"Isn't it incredible?" Zelda marveled. "Now, for sure, change will happen. The government simply must listen to us. The people have spoken!"

Flori wasn't as enthusiastic as her friend, nonetheless her heart filled with pride at what they were doing. As the crowd dispersed, she spotted Max and pushed her way through the masses to catch up with him.

"Hey Max!" She waved at him.

"Flori. What are you doing here?" Max immediately took her aside, shielding her from the people passing by.

"The same as you. Demonstrating for our rights."

"I never knew you had a rebellious streak. Even this past weekend you proposed more peaceful means." Taking her elbow, he guided her into an empty side street.

"I changed my mind. We workers have stayed silent for much too long. We need to show the SED how we really feel."

"Have you seen Katja?" Max suddenly asked.

"No. Why? Isn't she supposed to be at school?" A sudden suspicion sent cold shivers down her back.

"I met her friend Liese, who said Katja hasn't shown up for afternoon classes."

"You don't think Katja is protesting as well?" Flori asked, despite knowing this was exactly what Max suspected.

"If she is, she'll be fine. Even the police are on our side." Max's cheeks glowed with elation. "This is a new beginning for our country. You'll see, this is the breakthrough. Finally the people are heard."

"Let's go home." Suddenly, Flori was in a hurry, driven by the urge to find her sister safe and sound. She said goodbye to Max, making plans to walk to the strike with him the next morning. As she reached her apartment building, a man dressed in black with unruly blond hair was pacing up and down in front of it.

"Vladi! I'm so sorry!" She rushed up to him, profusely apologizing, because she'd completely forgotten that he was supposed to pick her up from work.

"Where have you been?" His lips contorted into a miffed pout.

"The chocolate factory workers decided to join the strike at Stalinallee. It was fantastic. You can't imagine how many people were there." Flori glowed with optimism.

"You participated in the illegal skirmishes against the government?" Vladi's face was a mask of shock.

"It's not illegal, on the contrary. There were thousands upon thousands gathered. Finally, we'll bring real change to our country." She beamed at him, chalking up his sour demeanor to the fact that she'd stood him up. "I'm sorry. With all the excitement I totally forgot that we were supposed to meet at the factory."

Finally, he smiled and kissed her cheek. "Can't you see how damaging these protests are, Floriane?"

"How can you say that? We, the people, must voice our concerns. You should have been there to see the spirit of optimism, the camaraderie, the willingness to improve our future..." Flori didn't want to argue with Vladi, so she said, "Do you want to come upstairs? I can make hot chocolate for us."

"I'd love to." Vladi's demeanor cheered up and he followed her to her apartment.

Disappointingly, Katja was home. "Hey Flori! Were you at the protests too? Great things are going to happen!"

"Yes, I was at Stalinallee. Such a fantastic atmosphere. You could feel the wind of change blowing." Flori forgot all about scolding Katja for skipping her afternoon classes. The future of their nation was much more important than some study group.

"Were you also at the demonstrations?" Katja asked Vladi.

"No, I wasn't. In fact, I think they are rather inappropriate. The government knows best how to lead the country. The workers are acting against their own best interests with this silly strike." Vladi's face didn't show a trace of a smile.

"Oh, come on, what are you? A Soviet asset or a Stasi spy?" Katja was much too bigmouthed for her own good. Watching how the vein in Vladi's temple pulsed, Flori jumped in to calm the waters.

"Vladi certainly doesn't work for the Soviets. He's a merchant for a company. Vladi, please excuse my sister's manners. She's in the middle of her final exams, which seems to have made her rather silly."

Behind Vladi's back, Katja stuck out her tongue at her sister, which Flori ignored. "I was about to make hot chocolate, do you want one too?"

"No thanks, I was about to leave. I'm going to meet with Liese."

Normally, Flori would have cautioned her not to hang out with the Christian girl, to avoid trouble, but since she yearned to be alone with Vladi, she kept silent. "Have fun."

Katja got up and embraced her sister, whispering into her ear, "Don't worry about me, I'll be out late. And use a condom."

Flori's cheeks burnt bright at the scandalous suggestion. Before she could answer, Katja had grabbed her jacket and sashayed out the door. Dumbfounded, she stared at the closed door, wondering whether her little sister was still a virgin.

When she turned around, Vladi stood there with a bemused smile on his lips. With two big steps forward, he took her into his arms. His tender kiss overwhelmed her, erasing all rational thought as she melted against his body. Forgetting everything around her, she felt an inexplicable unity with this man, clinging to him with unabashed joy and love.

CHAPTER 20

Vladi tenderly kissed Floriane. Making love to her had been a revelation. He knew everything about exquisite sex, yet he'd never before felt such an intimate connection to a woman. It was rather disconcerting to find that not only was his body attracted to her, but also his mind, heart and soul.

"Sleep well, sweetheart." He brushed his hand over her hair, reluctant to leave this woman who was spectacular, inside and out. Every cell in his body yearned to stay, to spend the whole night holding her in his arms. Alas, he had business to attend to.

"Will I see you tomorrow?" Floriane raised her angelic face, her lovely eyes full of trust sending a stab of guilt through his intestines. She'd made her opinion of Russians in general and, in particular, Soviet soldiers very clear. She might never fully trust him, if she knew…

Stop that thought right now, he admonished himself. He was not going to fall head over heels for a woman, even one as gorgeous as Floriane. She was but an interlude to sweeten his stay in Germany. Nice while it lasted, never meant to endure.

"Shall I fetch you from work?" he asked, devouring her luscious lips with his eyes. If there weren't an upheaval going on, he'd slip into bed with her once more to take both of them to unprecedented heights of ecstasy.

"I believe our factory is going to strike. Perhaps it would be better to meet someplace else?" Her eyes lit up. "Why don't you join us? The more the better."

Aghast at her scandalous suggestion, it took him a moment to get himself under control and speak in a calm voice. "I'm afraid that won't be possible."

"Don't you want our nation to become a better place?" Her hand snaked up his naked chest, evoking exquisite memories of their love making. To his own surprise it brought forth another emotion: the need to do everything in his power to make this woman happy.

"Naturally, I want this. I merely believe violence is the wrong way," he lied, since he usually wasn't opposed to using force on anyone deviating from the party line.

"You wouldn't say that if you had been there today. The atmosphere was so … joyful. The protesters weren't angry, no, quite the opposite, everyone was proud, knowing the importance of what we're doing."

Vladi was tempted to promise he'd join the demonstrations, for the sole reason of making her happy. "I'll see what I can do. In any case, I'll meet you at the corner pub around four p.m."

"That sounds good." She raised herself to sit, the bedsheet falling down and exposing her beautiful breasts to his gaze. He'd never desired a woman so much.

"I'll see you tomorrow, sweetheart." He kissed her lips, his tongue diving deep into her mouth, exploring every crevice. Exercising an inhuman amount of self-control, he kept his hands on her shoulders, not daring to venture downward or he'd be forever lost.

When he finally came up for breath, he said, "I'd love to stay, but I really need to leave."

"You should." She giggled. "My sister is due to come home any minute now."

It wouldn't be the first time he'd had two women in his arms –

sisters, friends or strangers. Strangely though, the idea now held no appeal. He wanted Floriane and no one else.

"Then I better get dressed." He stood up, stark naked, and walked toward the chair where he'd deposited his clothes, acutely aware of her admiring stare at his muscled backside. His heart raced with pure joy, an emotion more powerful than he'd ever thought possible. Could he be falling in love with this woman? Pushing this disturbing notion away, he made short work of getting dressed, and fled from the room.

Outside, he welcomed the chilly gusts of drizzly rain dampening his skin. The discomfort served to cool the hot, inner tempest caused by Floriane. Under no circumstance could he allow his personal life to interfere with the duty to his nation.

He hailed a cab, asking the driver to take him to the radio sender RIAS in the Western sector. Their hostile broadcasts were stirring up the protesters; not only in East Berlin but all over the nation. He hoped to convince Ernst Czarnowski, the director of RIAS, to stop pouring oil on the flames, and thereby pacifying the growing tension.

Entering the building, Vladi was met with a wave of chaos, much bigger than the usual bustle at radio or newspaper headquarters. People were rushing around, telephones ringing incessantly. He managed to wrestle his way through to Czarnowski's office, where he rapped on the open door.

"Come in." Czarnowski glanced up. "What do you want? We're busy."

"I'm on an official mission." Vladi frowned at the man's disrespectful manner.

Czarnowski snorted. "And you are…?"

He wished he was in uniform, before he remembered that Soviet soldiers were not supposed to cross into the West sector – an unwritten rule put in place since the unfortunate air circus instigated by the imperialists to counter an imaginary Berlin blockade, supposedly perpetrated by the Soviet Union.

"Vladimir Rublev, counselor to Norbert Gentner." He fished out his paper indicating he worked for the GDR government.

"Much afraid of real democracy, your so-called democratic government?" Czarnowski smirked, leaving Vladi reeling with disgust.

"I'm here to appeal to your sense of reason. The situation is explosive, due to your inflammatory reporting of a few minor skirmishes."

"Minor skirmishes, that's what you call them? To me, it looks more like the people flipping the bird at your dictatorial government."

It took all of Vladi's self-control to stay calm. "Whatever you like to call it, it's essential that you stop your coverage."

"Or what? Are you going to kidnap me and whisk me off to some Gulag in the Soviet Union?" Czarnowski didn't seem overly anxious at the prospect.

"Don't give me any ideas."

"You seem to have forgotten that this is the free sector of Berlin, backed by the free world."

Vladi wanted to slap himself for issuing a threat, which had caused the opposite effect he'd intended and made Czarnowski more rebellious. "Even in the free world, news has to be controlled for the people's wellbeing."

"That's not going to happen. What you've suggested is censorship, which is detrimental to the credibility and freedom of the press."

"Sometimes credibility has to take a step back to maintain order and prevent further chaos. We can't afford to have misinterpretations fueling the fire," Vladi retorted, his voice laced with frustration. "Look, I came here to advocate for peace. The GDR leadership does acknowledge the right of the workers to strike, but we need them to remain peaceful. Nobody wants a bloodbath, least of all the government."

"Sometimes sacrifices have to be accepted. I want this protest to succeed, to shake the foundations of power. Your government should tumble to the ground, for good!"

Vladi was taken aback by the audacity with which the journalist expressed his opinions. How could he be so reckless, so blinded by his own convictions? Why was he prepared to accept the possible death of protestors?

Since there was nothing more to be said or done to change Czarnowski's mind, Vladi bowed his head. "Any casualties will be on you and your imperialist warmongers."

Czarnowski guffawed. "Get out of my office, I have important things to attend to."

Shaking his head at the rudeness, Vladi abandoned his usual polite manners, leaving the office without a word of goodbye. He hailed another taxi to take him to the government buildings at Leipziger Strasse, eager to receive an update on the happenings on the street.

During the drive, his mind wandered to Floriane. Falling in love with her couldn't have happened at a more inopportune time. The nation was in turmoil and his superiors expected him to take any measures necessary to protect the stability and order of their socialist brother country. He simply could not afford to be distracted by emotions.

Still, he couldn't shake off the image of Floriane's loveliness and, more than once, he was tempted to ask the driver to change route to her apartment, where he would wrap her up in his arms. As always, duty won over his personal feelings and, minutes later, he stepped out onto the familiar asphalt, his shoulders sagging under the weight of his internal conflict.

Pushing aside his yearning for Floriane, Vladi stepped into the bustling atmosphere of the government building. The energy was palpable, a testament to the urgency of the situation and of the collective determination to find a resolution. Eager to pass on the responsibility for the crisis to someone else, he dispatched his report to Moscow, requesting further orders.

Then he joined the crisis meeting to give the government a summary of the situation on the street as well as his failed efforts with the enemy press. True to Czarnowski's vile promise, RIAS kept broadcasting vicious reports, inciting violence and encouraging more workers to join the protests. News of the strikes spread like wildfire throughout the GDR, creating an avalanche of support.

"Something has to be done," Norbert Gentner demanded.

"Currently, the situation is under control," the chief of police answered. "The protesters have gone home, peacefully. What I fear is a renewed flare-up in the morning, if the unions carry out their threat of a general strike."

"We cannot allow this to happen. If we give in to the demonstrators, our entire state is at stake. If the workers join forces with the Western imperialists, our nation is history and every single one of us will be ousted from power."

Vladi thought Norbert was being too dramatic. A simple protest surely wouldn't tempt the nation into deserting to the *Klassenfeind* - class enemy.

"Every year, close to two hundred thousand, mostly well-educated young citizens, are illegally leaving our nation to pursue their luck in West Germany. We must put a stop to this attrition," a minister said.

"Wouldn't agreeing to some of the workers' demands be the best way to take the pressure off the trend to emigrate?" another man suggested.

Norbert glared at him. "As I've already told Moscow, the New Course is the main driver of these protests. Easing up most of the strict measures is just begging for trouble."

"It's not helpful to shed your responsibility for this mess, pretending the Soviet Union has somehow caused it, when, in fact, we have done everything to support you throughout the past years." Vladi couldn't let anyone, not even a deputy prime minister, criticize the Kremlin.

Amidst this chaos, Vladi received an urgent call from Moscow.

"You've gotten yourself into quite a mess," boomed General Propov.

"I beg to differ, Comrade General," Vladi protested. "I've been sent here to watch and consult, not to take action."

Propov guffawed. "No need to get all worked up. The entire

leadership team has applauded your thorough report. Understandably, they are very concerned with the situation. It seems the protests are spiraling out of control."

"Comrade, I believe we still have the chance to suppress the riots. As we speak, the crisis team is meeting. As a first measure, the number of policemen has been doubled and the German army is on standby to move in wherever necessary. Our first priority is Berlin, although there are direct telephone lines set up to the regional authorities in all five states."

"Good." Propov paused, and Vladi could virtually see him twirling his mustache. From experience he knew to wait out his superior's silence. Just when Vladi feared the line had broken down, Propov continued. "With immediate effect, you're authorized to take whatever measures necessary to quash the uprising. This specifically includes calling in the Red Army."

An image of Floriane's body riddled with bullets sent shivers down his spine and he swallowed hard to compose himself. "Copy that: all measures authorized, including the deployment of the Red Army against the protestors."

"If the demonstrators succeed, this might spread like wildfire into other socialist countries. The Kremlin is counting on you not to allow this to happen."

"Understood, Comrade General." The burden of responsibility threatened to crush Vladi. He understood the order's severity and the potential consequences if he failed. Returning to the meeting room, a certain brunette slid into his thoughts, increasing the crushing weight on his shoulders.

Whatever happened the next day, he had to make sure Floriane stayed at her apartment where she would be safe.

CHAPTER 21

June 17ᵗʰ, 1953

E arly in the morning, Max got up. Throughout the night he'd been in meetings with union leaders, listening to the constant broadcasts of RIAS Berlin, which gave a clear picture about the situation in East Berlin, unlike the GDR broadcasters who didn't mention the day's events at all. The telephone lines at the office had run hot, coordinating activities, not only between unions in Berlin, but all over the country.

This would become huge. It was the opportunity they'd long been waiting for. Finally, the wind of change would blow through the archaic party, bringing honor to the name of the German Democratic Republic.

The people were going to stand up and speak for themselves, and the government had no choice but to listen.

He crossed the yard to Katja's and Flori's apartment block. Both of them had insisted they would participate in the protests. As much as Max wished to keep them away from possible harm, he couldn't, in good conscience, deny them the opportunity to join such a momentous event. Therefore, he'd opted for keeping them close. Just in case anything happened — which nobody seriously expected — he'd be able to protect the two most important women in his life.

Even before he knocked, the door sprung open. Katja stepped into his arms, her face beaming with excitement.

"This is it. We're finally doing away with arbitrary rules and injustice."

"Good morning to you, too, Katja." He pressed a quick kiss on her lips.

"I'm so excited. When the government sees how much we, the people, want change, they will have to oblige." Katja's eyes shone like a child's on Christmas Eve.

He chuckled. "My colleagues are of the same opinion, although nobody is jumping up and down the way you do."

"Good morning, Max." Flori stepped into his view. "Do I need a coat?"

"Probably. It's gray and muggy outside. There might be a thunderstorm later in the day."

"Do you have any idea of how much time the protest march will take?" Katja wrapped a light shawl around her shoulders.

"It really depends on the government. The union workers are prepared to strike until our demands are met." Late into the night, Max and his colleagues had been discussing possible outcomes. The majority agreed that the SED couldn't afford to ignore the will of the people and were going to offer negotiations. What his colleagues hadn't agreed on was the timeframe. The more optimistic ones suggested it would all be over by noon, while others warned the strikes might go on for at least a week until a common ground was reached. Max's expectations lay somewhere in the middle.

"Then, let's go." Katja linked arms with him and dragged him down the stairs, leaving her sister to lock the door and catch up with them.

He used the brief window of unobserved time to plaster a thick kiss on Katja's mouth, devouring her as if they hadn't seen each other in years. When he heard the main door click shut, he quickly released Katja, whose cheeks were flushed bright from the passionate kiss.

Looking at her, his heart burst with love, followed by a stab of fear. In the unlikely event that some protesters resorted to throwing stones or similar aggressive acts, he wanted to see her safe inside the walls of her apartment.

On the other hand, he was immensely proud of her willingness to fight for workers' rights, despite not having yet joined their ranks. It testified that this strike was going to be huge. Literally, *the people* were going to be on the streets in a peaceful protest for a better future.

They emerged from the underground at the closest station to the Stalinallee to find many thousands of men, women, and even children already gathered. Spotting his coworkers beside their construction site's entrance, he hastened his steps to catch up with them.

One of them unfolded a sign demanding the retraction of the increased production quota and handed one side to Max to carry. As they marched along the prestigious street toward the government buildings at Leipziger Strasse, elation took over.

Max had never felt so alive, so enthusiastic before. As a member of an expanding mass of like-minded people he marched, shouted slogans, chanted and chatted. By his side walked Katja, Flori, and his colleagues from the construction kombinat.

Not even the intermittent rain showers, drenching everyone to their bones, dampened the enthusiastic atmosphere. This was the workers' golden moment to urge for change and end the oppressive regime.

Approaching the government building, he noticed an increasing number of policemen gathering in clusters about the protesters. Even so, everyone kept calm, making Max immensely proud, because the police had to jump in if the march became violent, which might jeopardize the entire action.

Flori yelled, to be heard above the noise around them, "Look, there are my coworkers."

His gaze followed the direction of her arm, and he spotted Klara's brunette hair.

"Would you mind if I leave you to join them?" Flori asked.

"Not at all. Shall we arrange a meeting point for later?" Max asked. Flori was perfectly capable of returning to the apartment on her own, yet he wanted to make sure they could find each other again if needed.

"A good idea. At noon, 3 and 6 p.m. in front of the entrance to the historical museum?"

"Perfect. Then we can grab a bite somewhere. Take care." He gave her a quick hug, then sensed a tug on his other hand. He turned his head toward Katja, who looked at him with a questioning expression. "Can I stay with you?"

Flori looked surprised at this request. It must be hard to accept that Katja was growing up and wasn't considering her the most important person anymore. Max jumped right in to ease Flori's mind. "You might be better off with your sister and in a group of women."

Katja's glare was fierce as she answered, "I can take care of myself and I want to stay with you."

Before he had a chance to argue, Flori waved her hand. "It's fine with me. Take good care of her, Max, won't you?"

He nodded. He'd guard her like his own eyeballs.

CHAPTER 22

V ladi hadn't had a wink of shuteye all night.

He rushed to his accommodation in Karlshorst for a quick shower and a fresh set of underwear, before jumping into his uniform.

Downing a cup of strong coffee, he grabbed the latest reports, planning to read them in the car, before he gave Axel the address to Floriane's building.

"An informant?" Axel raised an eyebrow, since fraternization between Soviet soldiers and Germans was frowned upon.

"Not officially." Vladi had no intention of explaining himself. Letting the driver believe it to be a clandestine mission was probably best. He raced up the stairs, taking three steps at once and knocked on Floriane's apartment door, not caring that his uniform betrayed his identity.

The single thought on his mind was to warn her not to participate in the strikes today. No decision had been taken throughout the night, but one thing was clear: Norbert and the others wouldn't let power slip from their hands.

Vladi still hoped an escalation would be avoided by negotiating with the union leaders and granting slight concessions. Whatever happened, he didn't want Floriane to be in the thick of it, if a police deployment became necessary.

He stopped to listen, but no steps sounded inside. And no voice, either, asking for the identity of the knocker. After two more tries, Vladi turned around, clomping down the stairs in defeat, scolding himself for being too late. He should have swung by at the crack of dawn on his way to Karlshorst, instead of waiting for a more decent time.

Because there was no doubt that Floriane and her sister were on their way to join the protests. His heart squeezed with fear for the woman who'd captured his heart. Back in the car, he mused over the intensity of his emotions for Floriane, and he almost began weeping when he remembered the last woman he'd loved unconditionally with all his heart.

He'd been eighteen and had wanted to marry her. But Olga had been hauled away in the dead of night during Stalin's purges. Supposedly, she'd been a spy, though he knew better: the true reason was that she'd refused the advances of an important Kremlin official, because she loved Vladi.

Not knowing whether she'd been tortured, raped, and executed, or sent to a Gulag in Siberia, had almost cost him his sanity. The worst, though, had been the guilt: if Olga hadn't loved Vladi, she would have accepted the offer to become this man's mistress and would still be around. Almost twenty years later, he continued to consider himself responsible for her suffering. He'd sworn never to let a similar thing happen again. For all of his adult life he'd taken great care not to fall in love with another woman and –most importantly – not to let a woman truly love him.

He kept them at arm's length, making sure they understood a relationship with him was nothing but a fling, a noncommittal affair with no strings attached. So far, it had served him well, until Floriane had crossed his path and melted all the protective layers he'd built around his heart.

Why of all people did it have to be her? She was most unsuitable for a Soviet officer. Fear constricted his chest and he groaned. He could not, he would not, allow another woman to suffer because of him.

"Bad news?" Axel asked.

For a second, Vladi was confused, then he answered, "We'll have to see. Now, we better rush to the government building."

"Yes, comrade." Axel was a well-trained soldier, not asking unnecessary questions. He was probably also a spy, tasked to check on Vladi's loyalty for either the German or Soviet government, or both.

Having lived inside the Soviet military system from boyhood, he never completely trusted anyone, not even his father, the General, or his best friend, Grigori.

When they arrived at the government building, the hustle was even greater than the day before.

"Oh good, you're here." Norbert waved him over. "The reports we're getting are worrisome."

Vladi had seen for himself how small groups of workers walked the streets in direction of the Stalinallee, and assumed Floriane was among those who'd decided to demonstrate. Thus, his primary goal was to keep the protests peaceful, because the thought of her being harmed shredded his heart.

"On my way here, I saw some smallish crowds marching, all of them peaceful," Vladi mentioned, in an effort to play things down.

Norbert glared at him. "None of this is peaceful! If the workers were interested in a better future for the nation, they'd go to work and fulfill their production quota!"

"I agree," Vladi said, with a sour smile. He well knew that mindset from thirty plus years of socialization in the Soviet Union. For many years, he'd believed in Stalinism and everything that came with it, but recently doubts had crept into his mind. If their system truly was the morally superior one, why did so many people — when given a chance — decide to leave the system and pursue their luck in the West?

He rubbed his chin in thought. "While what you suggest is

obviously true, comrade, I wonder what might be the best way to disperse the protestors?"

"We must intervene swiftly and efficiently. I'm sending in police and German military."

"Wouldn't it be better to negotiate? I'm sure the crisis will wear itself out in a day at most, if you agree to one or two of the workers' requests."

"And risk setting a precedent? Showing weakness will only embolden them to demand more."

Vladi had no answer for this. The strict line had been favored for decades.

It turned out that police and military sympathized with the demonstrators and didn't act as brutally as they should have. Around ten a.m. the crowd had swelled further, and protests spread like wildfires across the entire nation, due to little resistance by the authorities and the provocative half-hourly broadcasts by the West Berlin radio station RIAS.

"We need to put an end to this nonsense, or the entire country will fall apart," Norbert roared.

But how? Vladi thought.

"You've already deployed the military. Why don't you give it a day or two?" Vladi desperately wanted to avoid any bloodshed.

"Because we don't have that much time. If we allow the anarchists to run wild, they'll cause havoc." Norbert squinted his eyes at Vladi. "What's your problem, Comrade Colonel? Why are you so against using harsher measures?"

"I'm not against it at all." Vladi raised his hands in defense; showing weakness could cost him his career. New Course or not, his superiors would not appreciate a full-blown rebellion in one of their vassal states. "I'm merely suggesting you give it some time to let the current measures take effect."

"On the contrary, we need immediate and decisive action to quash these troublemakers, or else the violence will inevitably get out of control."

CHAPTER 23

"This is so exciting," Flori gushed. All her colleagues had gathered: Klara, Helga, Carolin, Else, even grumpy Herr Schmidt. Together, they were marching for a better future. Born in 1929, she'd experienced the mass gatherings during Hitler's reign. Had marched with the *Bund Deutscher Mädel*, the German youth organization for girls. Had participated in military parades through Berlin. Had cheered at events hosting the speeches of Nazi leaders.

Today though, was different. This was a spontaneous gathering, not a carefully rehearsed event where everyone knew exactly when and how to cheer. This was very serious, people turning out on the streets for a better life. Nobody wanted to topple Socialism, or the government. Everybody wanted to work with their leaders to make the changes needed.

As they stood chanting, a heavy shower drenched them from head to toe. Flori was glad of her light coat, but even that couldn't withstand the rain for long and soon she was shivering in her wet clothes.

"I'm going home to get changed. You want to come?" Carolin asked.

Not willing to miss important developments, Flori shook her head. "No thanks. I'm fine."

"It's too far away for me, anyway," Klara said, linking arms with Flori. "We'll stay here. Don't want to miss the good stuff, do we?"

"We'll stay here until the very end," Flori reassured her friend. "Come back to us this afternoon."

"Fine. I have to make lunch for my children, but will return," Helga said, looking at Carolin. "What about you? "

Carolin flinched uncomfortably. "I guess."

Flori got the impression her friend was afraid, and wanted to reassure her. "There's no reason to be worried."

A voice droned through a megaphone, "Disperse. Please, everyone disperse."

Klara groaned. "As if that will help. Who do these people think they are?"

"The police maybe." Flori giggled.

The voice roared again, "This is an illegal demonstration. Please disperse. We don't want anyone to get hurt."

No one moved. If anything, the chanting got louder.

"What can they do? There's too many of us," Klara remarked.

"Right?"

The next second, she heard a gunshot. Flori instinctively ducked her head and asked in disbelief, "What was that? Did they really fire at us?"

"I think they shot into the air," Herr Schmidt answered.

Flori remembered the unmistakable sound of gunfire from the Battle of Berlin eight years ago and froze in horror. The trauma of the looting, murdering and raping by the Red Army troops, in the months following the occupation, was still raw, immobilizing her.

Another steady volley of bullets reverberated through the air, intensifying her fear. All around her, people scrambled to safety, while others hurled insults or stones at the police. Flori though, was incapable of moving, like a rock smashed by breaking waves except, unlike a rock, she wasn't immune to injury and pain.

A hand stole into hers. Klara's high-pitched voice penetrated through the fog in her brain. "Come on, we need to get away from the crowd."

Even as she was wondering how to do this, her feet moved of their own accord, stumbling after her friend, who apparently knew exactly what to do. To Flori, it seemed pandemonium had broken out, and with every breath the atmosphere became more charged, until she choked.

"Wait. I can't."

"Yes you can, and you will." Klara dragged her to the sidewalk. Once they'd freed themselves from the crowd, Flori managed to breathe again.

"Thank you."

From their vantage point she observed a few youths attacking police. The warning shots didn't deter them from aggressively clashing with the authorities they despised. Minutes later, black clouds of smoke hovered in the air, the stench of singed flesh burning in Flori's lungs.

Rumors spread that the Columbus House on Potsdamer Platz had gone up in flames. The crowd though, didn't seem to be frightened, on the contrary, the brutal attacks on their right to strike seemed to enrage the construction workers, most of them bulky, bullnecked men.

"I need to find Katja," Flori said, suddenly afraid for her sister.

"We can't possibly weave through this thick mass." Klara clung to Flori, shaking like an Aspen leaf.

"She's my little sister. I must find her." Cold shivers raced down Flori's spine as she observed the chaos unfolding in front of her, where not even buildings and infrastructure were spared from the rioters' fury.

"Why did they have to shoot?" Klara growled. "Everyone was peaceful and happy before the police intervened."

"This will not end well," Flori said, before a sense of rebellion overwhelmed her. "We must teach the government that they can't simply govern us as they please."

More shots rang through the air and the friends found themselves jostled and nearly knocked off their feet in the ensuing stampede.

"Come on, Klara!" Flori's voice pierced through the bedlam as she gripped her friend's hand tightly. "Run!"

Together, they ran until they came to a barricade, where they couldn't get through. Angry men torched a pile of broken furniture. Flames leapt up, igniting the blocked space, leaving no way out. Flori spied a spot still untouched by the flames and scaled up the debris, her grip on her friend's hand like steel as she dragged the struggling Klara upward.

"Hurry," she begged, her hoarse voice mixed with fury and sobs. "Come on, we must get out of here."

With a forceful shove, she pushed Klara over the jagged spikes and down the other side. Ignoring the pain coursing through her body, she pressed on without pausing to assess her bloody wounds.

Blazing fires cast an eerie glow across the chaos. With her heart pulsing fearfully and a determination to survive etched into her soul, Flori crouched behind a wall, watching the horrific scene unfold.

"I never expected anything like this," Klara whined. "Thank you for saving my life. My mind went blank and I froze. What would I have done without you?"

"You saved mine first. I simply returned the favor." Despite everything, Flori was still hopeful they'd get out of this unscathed. The optimistic atmosphere had vanished, replaced by an oppressive fear. She reckoned the riots were coming to an end. The crowd would calm down and things would return to normal. Then they could go home.

CHAPTER 24

The incoming news talked of bedlam. All over Berlin, rioters were clashing with the authorities, hurling projectiles, wielding makeshift weapons. Along the Stalinallee, windows were shattered, vehicles set ablaze, and even the Columbus house at Potsdamer Platz had gone up in flames.

The icy hand of fear grabbed Vladi's heart as more and more reports came in, presenting the same mayhem not only in Berlin, but all over the country. His greatest worry was to keep Floriane safe. Several times, he was tempted to escape from the government building and rush into the crowds on the street in search of her.

What stopped him was the futility of his endeavor. Searching for her amongst several thousand protesters, venting their anger and frustration, was not only foolish but also downright impossible. It was worse than searching for the proverbial needle in a haystack.

"There's more clashes at Alexanderplatz," one messenger announced.

"Two rioters dead in front of the university," another one said.

Vladi muttered a curse. None of this would have happened if Norbert hadn't lost his nerve. All the workers with whom Vladi had spoken, during the past few weeks, wanted improved working and living conditions, none were planning to overthrow the government.

Norbert had just thrown away the citizens' goodwill.

In response, they were now unleashing their anger in a tumultuous maelstrom of violence, directed at the political leadership who wouldn't listen to them.

Unfortunate as it was, the shit had hit the fan and strict measures must be imposed. Vladi steeled himself for what he knew was inevitable. For one last time, he imagined Flori's sweet face, her trusting eyes, blaming himself for not having swung by her apartment earlier that morning to ensure her protection.

Another thought crossed his mind: She'd been so enthusiastic about the strikes, wanting a better future for her nation.

Cursing Norbert Gentner and the entire GDR government once more, he bit on his lips, dismissing Flori's image. After the riots were over, he'd find her and see what he could salvage of their relationship.

Right now he had to obey the duty to his country, which always came above anything else.

Raising his voice, he said, "You have failed miserably."

Heads turned, and wide eyes stared at him, filled mostly with fear, but including a sliver of hope that, like a mother, he'd come to their rescue.

"This catastrophe is entirely the fault of your mishandling of the situation." Vladi absolutely had to distance himself from any personal involvement and put the blame for the fiasco on someone else, while trying to rescue what was left.

Norbert's expression twisted with a blend of anger and contempt, his brows furrowing deeply like the trenches of a war-torn battlefield. He dismissed Vladi's analysis with a derisive snort.

Adrenaline coursed through Vladi's veins, alerting his senses, propelling him into a state of high alert. This might well be the last showdown and, depending on the outcome, he might either be awarded a promotion or be sent to Siberia. In terms of rank, the deputy prime minister stood way above him. But Vladi possessed the backing of the country ultimately pulling the strings.

"This was a peaceful protest before you blew it. A savvier politician would have satisfied the workers with a few minor concessions, then retracted them a few weeks or months later."

"You, of all people, suggest diplomacy and empathy?" Norbert thundered, his voice brimming with scorn. "You have the audacity to question my judgment, comrade? When has Stalin ever been mellow or wavering?"

"The great Stalin is dead. New leaders have new ways. You and I, we merely follow their rules." Vladi had been trained not to question orders. Whether he approved of the New Course or not was irrelevant.

His words had the desired effect, because a streak of fear entered Norbert's defiant expression.

"So, what do you suggest we do? Negotiate with the rioters?" Norbert asked, the slightest trace of a sneer in his voice.

"It's too late for that. We have to send in the military."

"We already did that, if you care to remember."

Vladi took his sweet time looking at each of the attendants. "You deployed *your* military, not ours."

The German politicians gasped as each of them considered the enormity of his suggestion. It would undermine the sovereignty they'd been grappling for and show to friend and foe alike that the men in charge were nothing but puppets of a bigger power. On the other hand, it was the only way to keep them in power.

Vladi watched the truth trickling into the brains of these men. The change in their facial expressions pinpointed the exact moment when each one realized the quagmire they'd maneuvered themselves into.

Finally, Norbert broke the silence. "Send the Red Army."

Vladi nodded and walked toward the red telephone, which had established a direct line to the Kremlin. It took less than five minutes to receive the approval he sought.

Then, Vladi turned toward the commanding officer of the Soviet troops stationed in Germany. "General, Moscow wants you to send in the tanks."

Handing the receiver to the general, Vladi's gut churned at the image of his beloved Floriane crushed under the chains of a tank. True to Soviet doctrine, he'd never believed in God, but now he sent a prayer to the heavens to keep her safe.

With the problem out of his hands, he returned to his lodgings for a change of clothes.

CHAPTER 25

A deep rumble alarmed Flori. Craning her neck, she finally saw the origin of the sound and blanched. "They've sent tanks."

Klara tried a chuckle. "That's not funny. Our nation doesn't even own tanks."

The rumble intensified. Seconds later, outraged cries bellowed through the air, "Those bastards! They've deployed the Red Army!"

A powerful deja vu chilled Flori to the bone as she observed the tanks, each with a red star painted on the side, rolling down the street just as they had at the end of the war. Back then, a time of utter and complete horror had descended on the city until, two months later, the Americans had arrived and brought some semblance of law and order with them.

A second later, absolute mayhem broke out, as the crowd scrambled for safety. All around her was shouting, panting, screaming, and the threatening growl of the tanks moving forward.

Beside her, Klara cried out in anguish. Flori grabbed her hand tight. Whatever happened next, she did not want to face it without her friend by her side.

"We have to get away!" Flori shouted.

"But how?" Klara glanced around her. "The tanks are everywhere.
"

The mass frenetically pushed in the direction of Potsdamer Platz, and the two women stumbled with them. More shots were fired. Beside her someone screamed, grabbing his bleeding shoulder with an expression of disbelief.

Before Flori could comprehend this, she was pushed forward, her only goal to avoid being trampled to death. Frantically searching for a way out, she racked her brain to decide whether it was safer in the middle of the frantic group or at the fringes, where the tanks drove.

"There!" She spotted a gap in the chain of vehicles at the entrance of a small alley.

Klara must have seen it too, because she wrestled her way through the onslaught of bodies going the other way, dragging Flori behind. Flori's heart hammered wildly against her ribs, as she stumbled, pushed, jumped, and wrestled until they reached the side of the street, where the tanks were moving along. Slow, thundering, atrocious.

Waiting for an opening between two vehicles, they finally raced through to the relative safety of the small alley, away from the pushing masses and out of reach of the threatening tanks.

"Oh my God, I believed for sure we'd die in there." Flori doubled over, regaining her breath. When she straightened up again, the air around her crackled with tension, and she had to force herself to keep calm and think. She gazed around, attempting to orient herself. "Isn't that the university down there?"

"It is." Klara nodded at her. "We could follow this alley to get there."

"Good idea." Flori was about to turn around when her eyes fell upon a group of young men on the side of the main road, crossing through the line of tanks the way she and Klara had done a minute earlier. One of them stumbled and fell flat on his face.

"Stop!" a dozen voices roared as one; yet the tank driver could not hear them in his metal container, neither could he see.

The fallen man's friend scrambled to grab his hands to heave him up. But it was too late. The huge chains caught first his foot and then squashed the rest of him, while the helping friend continued to hold his hand, staring at the scene in horror, until someone dragged him out of danger.

Flori shut her eyes tight, because she did not want to witness the ghastly reality of the scene.

"Let's go." Klara, visibly trembling with terror, tugged at her hand.

Not able to think clearly, Flori succumbed to her friend's lead, only waking from her stupor when they'd reached the end of the side alley and stepped onto another main street. This one featured no Soviet tanks lining the sides.

A surprising scene greeted them. Rather than thinning out, this street was alive with protesters pouring in from every side, their determined voices echoing through the square and beyond. Flori found hope again. She and Klara marched with the crowd up to the university, where a makeshift podium had been erected, with students clamoring for freedom of speech. Her stomach lurched as she believed she saw her sister up there, exposed to the wrath of the police.

"What are we going to do?" Klara asked.

"We stay and protest, of course." With no tanks in the vicinity, Flori found her courage again.

"I had no idea this would be so huge!" Klara's voice betrayed her astonishment.

"It's fantastic, isn't it?" Ever so slowly, her enthusiasm returned.

"Have you noticed the number of people flooding in? Looks like newcomers are joining the protest; there are hordes of them...where are all these people coming from?"

"Plenty of West Berliners have joined our cause," a woman next to them said.

"Despite the Soviets sending in tanks?" Flori asked her.

The other woman, of a similar age, with long, curly blonde hair, raised her eyebrows. "Tanks? Where?"

"We've just escaped them over on Stalinallee."

A flicker of fear crossed the woman's face, then she shrugged. "They can't kill us all. We're too many."

Flori desperately wanted to believe her.

Up there on the stage, ringleaders were calling for change. Emboldened by the masses cheering them on, they refused to back down, even as soldiers mounted the podium and ordered them to disperse.

Then, in front of thousands of witnesses, more soldiers arrived, arresting the students and hauling them away. A sinking feeling washed over Flori, knowing justice itself had been punched between the eyes.

One of the soldiers snatched the megaphone and shouted into the gathered crowd, "Disperse. This is our final warning - anyone who hasn't left the square in five minutes will be arrested."

The woman next to Flori laughed. "They can't arrest us all."

Suddenly, a wave of movement rippled through the crowd. Shots rang out, tearing through the air with a deafening roar. Panic and chaos erupted, as people scattered in all directions, their courage dripping from their souls like blood from an oozing wound.

The casualties of indiscriminate fire littered the streets and sent shockwaves through the crowd. Cries of pain and anguish pierced the air. The once-united brave front of protesters scattered, their ranks broken and fragmented by the brutal force unleashed upon them.

Flori found herself pushed toward a corner of the square, gripping Klara's hand for dear life. But just before they came upon a row of soldiers, they were separated. Klara drifted in one direction, herself in the other. Much as she struggled, there was no way to resist the collective momentum. Seconds later, she stood eye to eye with a soldier.

"You're under arrest," he stated, while he efficiently twisted her arms up her back and then handcuffed her.

"I haven't done anything wrong!" she screamed in panic.

Her pleading fell on deaf ears and she was pushed and pulled into a side alley, and then into a waiting van. Inside, she was greeted by anguished faces of men and women, old and young. When the van was full, the doors were slammed shut, and it sped away to some unknown place.

Flori's only hope now was that Klara had witnessed the abduction and would come looking for her.

CHAPTER 26

By late afternoon, the rebellion was history. Since his presence wasn't needed any longer, Vladi left the government building to check upon Floriane. He decided to walk, because he wanted to see the evidence of the happenings firsthand — and he needed time to think about how to explain to the woman he loved so much that quashing the protest had been for the best.

Nobody had wanted to employ extreme force, least of all Vladi. But the workers had proven unreasonable, continuing to protest even after warning shots were fired. When one local revolt was put down, another erupted elsewhere. When one protester fell, another took his place; if many fell or gave up, still more kept coming.

Stepping across the debris, Vladi reflected upon the similarities of the sight that greeted him today with the Battle of Berlin eight years ago. In the end, the heroic Red Army had won, like they always did. The combatants might be out of practice because so much time had passed since the war, nevertheless, they had delivered.

The protesters were silenced. Only the debris littering the city was left to show the attempt of an unruly population, to overthrow their rightfully elected government. According to the reports coming into headquarters, foolish students had thrown stones at the tanks and tried to stop the vehicles with poles and boards. As if such mighty war machines could be stopped with bare hands.

When darkness descended, a cemetery-like atmosphere spread across the city. The crowds had dispersed and the sector borders were closed. A strict curfew was imposed. Anyone showing their face in the streets risked arrest.

Vladi strode along the empty roads, passing Soviet soldiers lighting bivouac fires in the open, as they had done during the war, settling in for the night. Guilt poisoned his soul, not allowing him to feel any pride at the successful oppression of the strike. He had done his duty, had obeyed the demands for the greater good, but for some strange reason he felt sympathy for the German workers, for whom the day had begun so hopefully and had ended in such tragedy.

Vladi knew what was about to happen: many more would be arrested and punished with long prison sentences, after signing a confession tortured out of them.

Just a few weeks prior, Beria had officially condemned the use of physical torture on prisoners. In the end that only meant the methods had changed to ones which wouldn't leave any marks, except on the soul or in the mind, where they couldn't be seen. Vladi pitied any person caught up in the inevitable clean up.

He reached Floriane's building and rushed up the stairs, knocking on her door. Her sister Katja opened, recoiling when she recognized the uniform.

"Is Floriane home?" he asked.

"No, she's not." Katja gazed up at him, her eyes widening. "Aren't you…?"

"Yes, I'm her friend Vladimir Rublev. Where is she?"

Her piercing glare seemed to stab daggers at him. Her fearful voice turned hostile as she answered, "You have some nerve showing up here!"

A knot of apprehension tightened his chest. "What has happened?"

"Do you really have to ask? All of this is your fault!" Distress etched her face as tears threatened to spill down her cheeks. Her voice boomed in the long corridor and he sensed the neighbors edging closer to their doors, no doubt peeking through their peep holes, not wanting to miss the scene.

"May I please come in?" He didn't wait for an answer, but instead moved toward her, gently nudged her inside and closed the door behind them. "Please, tell me what has happened."

"You…you…vicious bastard!" Without any forewarning, she took a step toward him and slammed her fist into his chest.

Too surprised to react, he allowed her to pummel into him for several seconds, before he grabbed her wrists and held them high into the air. "Calm down, will you?"

"No, I won't. I hate the Soviets. I hate you. Wasn't it enough to suppress our nation? No, you had to come with your tanks and kill us all." Her spluttered words made no sense.

"Where is your sister?" he asked again, hoping to get a coherent answer from her.

"Your friends have arrested her!" she spat at him, her eyes crazed. The words tumbling from her trembling lips pierced his soul.

The shock chilled him to the bone; images of sweet Floriane hanging from the gallows making him gag. He had to prevent her from being sent to the political prison in Hohenschönhausen, because even his power ended outside those gates. Another shudder raced down his spine as he remembered Zara, a woman who'd been released from there after three weeks in the hands of the NKVD. Under no circumstances would he allow the same to happen to Floriane.

If he wanted to save her, he had to act fast.

"When and where?" he barked at Katja, harsher than he'd planned.

The effect, though, was immediate. She straightened her shoulders and said flatly, "In front of the university at around four p.m."

"Were you with her?" he asked, in a much softer voice.

"No. Her friend, Klara, swung by to let me know."

Ignoring her shivering frame, he persisted, "Is there anything else you know? Anything that might help to find her?"

"No." She shook her head. He watched how the last bit of energy whooshed out of her, and she collapsed onto the sofa. "What are they going to do to her?"

"Nothing, if I can prevent it."

"You?" She shrugged listlessly. "You're one of them. Your tanks crushed our hope, along with so many lives."

The burden of guilt threatened to crush him. Katja had no idea how right she was. He had been the one to deploy the tanks. If he'd known that Floriane would get hurt... *You'd still have done it,* an inner voice reminded him. *Your conscience is clean. You were only doing your duty.*

But, deep down, he knew he'd never forgive himself if Floriane was seriously harmed, because he had sworn that never again would another woman be injured because of him.

"I'm going to get her out."

"But how?"

He didn't want Katja to know that he had no idea. "Don't worry, I'll find her." Just as he was about to open the door, he turned around and said, "Don't tell anyone or you might jeopardize her liberation."

"I won't." She seemed to struggle with herself. Then she said, "Thank you."

CHAPTER 27

T he van stopped. Everyone was ushered out and ordered to
separate into men and women. Flori shielded her eyes against
the sudden light streaming into the completely dark van. Stumbling
behind the others, she found herself in a group of women next to a
much larger one of men.

Before her eyes had time to fully adjust to the light, they were led
away. As far as she could tell, she was inside a prison yard,
surrounded by high brick walls. Then she was shoved
unceremoniously into a cell that already overflowed with people.

The dim light filtering through the glass block window was barely
enough for her to distinguish between the other women in her cell.
She shivered violently – although not from cold, because the many
bodies heated the cell almost unbearably high. There was no place to
sit down, so she kept standing, curiously eyeing her fellow prisoners.
They seemed similar to herself: workers, housewives, students. None
of them looked like criminals.

"Do you know where we are?" she asked the woman next to her,
who simply shrugged.

"Were you at the protests, too?" Flori asked again.

"Better stop asking so many questions," a stout woman behind
her said, her hostility palpable.

Since no one seemed keen on trying to connect or was even curious enough to find out where they were, Flori resigned herself to silence. The minutes and hours passed, and nothing happened. Her grumbling stomach was a reminder that she hadn't eaten anything since breakfast this morning, and she wondered what time it was.

She swallowed down the curiosity once more, because it was too dark to decipher the time on her wristwatch, and she didn't dare to ask. Desolation settled deep in her soul, as she feared she'd never leave this place.

After what seemed like an eternity, the door opened and bowls of soup were distributed to the hungry women. It was a disgusting, thin gruel, yet Flori devoured it, relieved to quench her raging thirst.

Several women were taken away and she finally found an empty space to sit down, where she must have fallen asleep, because she started at the screeching sound of the door. A guard entered, yelling, "Floriane Eilers."

It took her a few seconds to process who he meant. Then she jumped up. "That's me."

The guard's serious face didn't give away why she was summoned. Flori's initial elation turned into pure panic as she followed him through long corridors without meeting another living soul. She itched to turn on her heel and run.

"Stand with your face to the wall. Don't move," the guard ordered.

A thousand ants ran down her spine as she stood motionless, her nose inches away from the yellowed wallpaper, waiting for his next command. The sound of shuffling feet to her left caused her to slightly crane her neck, just to feel his heavy hand on her head as he reminded her, "Face to the wall."

More shuffling steps. The clinking of a door presumably opening and closing. Then silence again. Rigid with fright she did not move a single muscle, except for her ferociously hammering heart, though she felt she could faint at any moment.

"Turn around." The guard's voice was maddeningly neutral. For a second, she wished he'd lash out at her, just so she knew he was a human being with emotions. At the end of the corridor he stopped in front of an open lattice door. "Inside."

Every cell in her body protested against the command. Still, she put one foot in front of the other, feeling as if she were a wild animal walking into a trap. Goosebumps broke out all over her skin, in spite of the warm temperature.

As soon as she'd passed the lattice door, she heard the guard close and lock it behind her. Unsure whether she was allowed to move, she stayed frozen in the middle of the small room, until his next command came, as cold as the ones before.

"Get undressed."

Blushing furiously from head to toe, she turned around to protest, only to stare into an empty corridor, the guard vanished from sight.

The peculiar cell was actually a part of the corridor, separated by a see-through grid of thick iron poles. The windows were of the same glass blocks as the ones in the previous cell, dimming the light filtering through them. Except, here a naked bulb hung from the ceiling, bathing the cell in a strong, glary light, almost as if floodlights shone on her.

On the left and right walls were radiators, explaining the warmth in the cell. Next to one of them stood a clothes hanger. The prospect of having to face the guard, stark naked, twisted her stomach with shame.

There was nothing she could do. Alone in the cell, she couldn't find the courage to resist, and what would have been the chance of success, anyway? If her captors decided she was to be deprived of her modesty, they surely had other ways to make her comply if she didn't cooperate willingly.

With trembling hands, she stepped out of her shoes and stockings, putting them next to the radiator on the floor, then she took off her dress, hanging it neatly on the coat rack. She was nervously fumbling with her bra, when she heard footfalls approach.

Instantly, she froze in place, fearfully expecting to see the returning guard. Her relief was immeasurable when two females came to a standstill in front of the bars.

"Hurry up, I don't have all day," one woman hissed at her, before she pressed a button on the other side of the corridor – well out of reach for anyone inside the cell—and the lattice door opened to let the other woman through. Like a crowded animal, Flori shrank back into the corner.

"Get undressed," the guard commanded, as she pulled plastic gloves over her hands.

Somehow, Flori managed with trembling fingers to pull down her undergarments and hang them on the rack under the watchful eyes of the two women. Completely naked, exposed not only to the two guards, but also to anyone who might pass along the corridor, she shivered despite the warmth.

"Face to the wall. Spread your legs," the woman ordered, her voice as maddeningly impersonal as the male guard's tone had been. Then she proceeded to pat her down before she eased her fingers into all of Flori's openings, thoroughly feeling for hidden objects.

It was easily the most embarrassing treatment in Flori's entire life. Every cell in her body burnt hot with shame and she wished she'd never been born.

"She's clean," her tormentor announced to the other guard waiting outside.

Flori sagged with relief, since her ordeal apparently was over. Taking a step away from the wall, she sensed cold metal on the skin of her back.

"Don't move until you're ordered to."

Swallowing hard, she froze.

"Step back to the wall and put your palms against it."

Flori did as she was told. She heard the soft clink when the door opened and the guard stepped outside. The door shut again even before the thought to flee had a chance to cross her mind. Every procedure in this place was designed to efficiently prevent disobedience, unrest or escape.

"You can get dressed now," the first woman said, watching Flori as she recovered her modesty. After the procedure was done, she was led away through long, lonely corridors to a solitary cell, where she spent the night.

Late the next day, she was taken to some kind of reception area, where a man in Soviet officer's uniform waited for her. Her first instinct was to scream in panic, but when he turned around, she had the fiercest urge to scratch out his eyes.

"This is the prisoner you want? Floriane Eilers?" some official asked.

"Yes, it's her. I have orders to transfer her to the SCC headquarters for further interrogation," Vladi answered, shooting her a warning glance.

Even if she had wanted to, she wouldn't have been able to utter a single word, so strong was her emotional turmoil. She felt betrayed, used, and frightened, all at the same time, but also gained a sliver of hope as she looked at the man she'd thought she loved.

"Let's go." He nodded at her.

"Do you need help?" The receptionist's question earned him a bemused smirk from Vladi.

"Do you doubt I'll be able to deal with this woman?"

"Of course not, Colonel," the official quickly stammered.

Gripping Flori's upper arm, Vladi strode outside toward a government car waiting in the yard. He pushed her into the passenger seat and then settled behind the steering wheel, not uttering a single word. Unsure what to expect and wondering whether she'd jumped out of the frying pan and into the fire, Flori kept silent, too. Her heart raced as the enormity of his betrayal dawned on her. The man she'd fallen in love with was not who he'd pretended to be.

He was indeed Russian, a Soviet Army officer no less, and had lied to her all along. The realization sent shockwaves through her, shattering the trust she had placed in their relationship. For all she knew, he might not even have feelings for her.

As soon as the prison gates had closed behind them, Vladi turned his head and hissed, "Didn't I tell you to keep away from the strikes, you foolish woman?"

The harsh words caused indignation to banish her fear and she hissed right back at him, her voice trembling with a mixture of anger and hurt, "You lied to me! All this time, all those sweet words...was any of it real?"

"Of course it was." Hurt shone in his eyes and his voice softened with affection. "Don't you realize how much I care for you? I wouldn't be here otherwise. It's a considerable risk for me, if anyone finds out."

"Your people sent in the tanks."

Vladi's face turned into a stony mask, as if he was keeping something from her, but she had no time for this now, since she still struggled to comprehend what had happened. "You mowed down the population of your socialist brother nation. Why would the Soviets do this?"

"It was your own government which called for help," Vladi replied.

"I don't believe you!" she cried out. "How am I ever again going to trust a single word of yours?"

Vladi's expression wavered between guilt and exasperation. He reached out to touch her arm, making her recoil, refusing to let him comfort her.

"Floriane, please, let me explain," he pleaded, his voice tinged with regret. "I never wanted to deceive you. I care deeply for you, and I thought...I thought we would get to know each other first..."

Flori narrowed her eyes. "Were you ever going to tell me?"

He shrugged listlessly.

"How can I ever believe anything you say? If you were capable of lying about something as fundamental as your nationality and your profession, what else are you hiding from me?" She stopped talking, because she didn't trust herself not to break down in tears and didn't want to give him this satisfaction.

"I don't know," he admitted, barely able to meet her gaze. "Please, believe me when I say that my feelings for you are real. I never meant to hurt you. This is why I got you out of jail."

"And now you expect me to fall at your feet with gratitude?" He didn't have to know that she was immensely thankful to be freed from the awful prison and would have licked his boots if he'd asked her to.

"I...I don't know what to say. I couldn't stand the thought of you being imprisoned, knowing what would await you there. Please, Floriane..." he turned to gaze into her eyes with a disconcerting intensity, "...you are in great danger and must leave the country."

"Excuse me?" Her brain hurt from the many experiences of the past days. "You got me out, I'm free now."

"I got you out, because of my uniform, which you seem to hate so much. Since I was acting without official orders, the authorities might capture you again and I won't be able to come to your rescue a second time," Vladi said, his voice soft as velvet.

Flori very much wanted to believe him, wanted to snuggle up to him, feel the comforting rub of his fingers across her back, yet she resisted. He had lied to her. Not once, but for weeks on end. "Can you drive me home, please? I need time to think."

"As you wish. I'll return in the morning to look for you. Please promise to consider leaving the country. It's not safe anymore for you."

When he stopped in front of her building, she looked at him for a few seconds, willing her pain away, trying to objectively assess his motive in liberating her from prison.

"Thank you," she finally said. "I'll wait for you in the morning." Then she gave him a last wave and turned her back on him, entering the building.

CHAPTER 28

Not long after Vladi had left to find Flori, another knock came on the door. Expecting Max, Katja jumped up and opened it. One of his coworkers stood in front of her, turning his cap in his hands, his expression solemn.

"What's wrong?" Katja's voice was screechy, even to her own ears.

"Can I come in, please?" Hans asked.

Her knees threatening to give out under her, she stabilized herself against the wall as she nodded. The way this man looked at her sent icy chills into every cell of her body.

"I'm so sorry…" he began, interrupted by her high-pitched scream. "… Max is dead."

Then, everything around her went dark and she came to, half-lying, half-sitting on the sofa Max had built from a couple of old boxes. Her Max. She violently shook her head, demanding, "Tell me it's not true."

"It is. I was standing next to him when it happened."

An unreasonable anger at Hans boiled her blood. Balling her hands into tight fists until the fingernails cut deep into the flesh of her palms, she wished it had been him who'd been killed and not her beloved Max. Just when they had finally confessed their deep love for each other, their happiness had been brutally destroyed.

Strangely, no tears pooled in her eyes. Apart from the pain in her hands, the only feeling was emptiness. A big, black hole, threatening to consume her.

"Tell me how it happened," she whispered.

"There was an altercation, some youngsters throwing stones at the soldiers. They fired warning shots. A stray bullet hit Max in the head. He died a minute later in my arms."

Another wave of darkness swept over Katja and, for a second, she wanted to follow Max to whichever place he was in now.

"Katja…" Hans' voice reached her through the depths of the darkness, "…his last word was your name. He loved you."

"I loved him too. So much." Still no tears came.

Hans patted her hand. "I need to go home. Will you be alright?"

Despite knowing she'd never be alright, ever, in her entire life again, she nodded.

Apparently not believing her, he looked around the apartment. "Where's Flori?"

"In prison."

"Oh dear." His expression was full of shock. "Do you want to stay with us for a while? I'm sure my wife won't mind."

She shook her head. His offer was very kind, but she didn't want to be with strangers right now.

"I want to be here, in case Flori is released."

"Alright." By the way he looked at her, it was clear he thought her delusional for hoping her sister might be freed anytime soon. "If you need anything, you know where to find me."

"Thank you so much." Suddenly, she couldn't wait to get him out of her home, for she needed to be alone with her grief.

The moment she locked the door behind him, she collapsed to the floor and turned into a blubbering mess of tears. She sat there motionless for hours, bawling her eyes out until no more tears came.

Then, she got up and opened the window to let in fresh air. Night had fallen over the city. Apart from a few flickers of orange, cast by remaining fires, the sky was completely black, shrouded with heavy clouds, as if grieving over all the senseless deaths on the day that had started so cheerfully.

Without thinking, she climbed onto the windowsill, mysteriously drawn to the void beneath it. It would be so easy to throw herself down the three stories to end her pain. Only the hope of Flori returning, due to Vladi's involvement, made her stay where she was, crouched against the window frame, whimpering like an injured animal.

"Murderers!" she screamed into the night, reliving the agony of losing her parents, her brothers and so many of her friends, all over again. For eight years she'd carefully locked the grief inside her soul, had eked out an existence, even happiness with Flori and Max. Until at last, fate had caught up with her like a cat on the prowl.

Stoically, she awaited the final blow, the paw swipe under which she'd finally be crushed for good. When it didn't materialize, she climbed down from the windowsill and crawled to the sofa, where she fell asleep. The next morning, she slept through the incessant ringing of the alarm clock and only woke up in the late afternoon when the door opened, and Flori walked in.

"Good heavens, what has happened here?" Flori yelped.

"Are you a ghost?" Katja asked, her mind shrouded in sorrow.

"No. It's me in the flesh, but you look like the living dead yourself." Flori settled next to her on the sofa, her inquiring gaze meeting with Katja's. Flori rubbed her hands across her sister's hair. "Tell me what happened, sweetie."

"Max is dead." Those three words were enough for her raw emotions to break the dam and tears ran down her cheeks again, followed by heartbroken sobs.

"I'm so sorry." Shock clouded her features. "Poor Max."

"Poor me," Katja whined. After all, Max was dead and she was left to endure the emotional torment.

"Don't say that. You're still alive."

"I was so desperate last night without the two of you."

"Now I'm here and we'll get through this together."

Guilt washed over Katja for her selfish behaviour. After all, her sister had loved Max like a brother. Gathering her remaining strength, she said, "Vladi found you?"

"How do you know?"

"He came here looking for you. When I told him that you'd been arrested he promised to use his connections to free you. But, since Klara couldn't tell me where they'd taken you, he first had to find you." She cast a suspicious glance at Flori, before she asked, "Did you know he was a Soviet officer?"

"No. He lied to me. If I'd known, I would never have..." Flori blushed furiously.

"Oh my God. You slept with him?" Katja's hand flew to her mouth.

"I did." Flori was a picture of misery.

"How was it?" Katja couldn't resist being nosy. As far as she knew, her older sister had only had two or three boyfriends, but never done it with them. Flori had also never confided what the Russian soldiers had done to her after the war, although by piecing together bits and pieces from different sources, Katja had a clear picture of the ordeals most women had endured at the hands of the conquerors – before they'd pretended to be friends and brother nations.

A lie exposed a day ago, when they'd sent their tanks against unarmed people, protesting peacefully for more democracy.

Flori's face took on a dreamy expression. "It was fantastic. He was so tender and caring...I experienced sensations I never knew existed."

"He seems to love you. He was truly disturbed at the news of your arrest."

"Now that I know who he is, there can never be anything between us." Flori pressed her lips together.

"Why not?" A week ago, Katja would have wholeheartedly disapproved of the relationship, but the tanks had changed everything. The thin screen of pretend-democracy had fallen; the government had shown its true colors. She might only be a recent high school graduate, but experience told her, with certainty, that henceforth the leaders, with the help of their Soviet overlords, would double down on oppressing anyone or anything in favor of more freedom.

"Because he's our enemy." Flori seemed to have come to the same conclusion.

"He liberated you. Having him as a boyfriend will probably have many benefits."

"What do you take me for? A Russian whore?"

"Don't be silly. You're in love with him, there's nothing wrong with that."

"There's a lot wrong with it. Beginning with the fact that he lied to me about being a Russian."

"I get it. He lied to you. You know how opposed I was to your relationship with him, don't you?" Katja felt herself blush at the memory of how she'd pummelled her fists into his chest when he came to ask for Flori. "He must truly love you though, because he's risked a lot to free you."

"That doesn't undo his betrayal. He lied, period. And he's a Red Army officer. He could have been the one sending the tanks. Who knows, he might have fired shots at the crowd as well."

"You're exaggerating. Didn't he prove his intentions by getting you out of jail?" Having just lost the love of her life, she didn't want Flori to throw her chance of happiness away.

"Let's not talk about this." Flori hunched her shoulders. "Do you want a hot chocolate?"

"I really could use one." Hot chocolate was a proven remedy against all kinds of ailments, ranging from a cold or a scratched knee, to the agony of a broken heart. Today though, Katja feared it wouldn't be able to ease the horrid pain Max's death had left in her soul.

When Flori returned with two steaming mugs of Vitalade, she said, "Vladi urged me to leave the country."

"Why's that?" Slowly sipping the hot liquid, Katja scrutinised her sister's expression, waiting for an answer.

"He said it's not safe. The Stasi might arrest me again and then he won't be able to help."

Katja leaned back to process the information, reflecting about the implications. Vladi's assertion made sense. After being released from prison, Flori's name was probably on some kind of watch list, where even the slightest misstep was severely punished. After a long silence, she said, "I'm coming with you."

"What?" Flori seemed to have forgotten the topic they'd been talking about.

"To West Germany."

"You're not seriously considering escape? It's illegal." In spite of her recent arrest Flori still seemed to care about law and order.

"It's also illegal to murder peaceful protesters," Katja stated dryly, swiping the brimming tears away.

"That was...those were...I mean...the Soviets did that."

"You must be aware that our government asked them for help. Even if they didn't, one thing is for sure: starting immediately, the Soviets are tightening the leash. We'll never be free."

CHAPTER 29

"We did it!" Norbert accepted the vodka his wife proffered. "Yes, we did it." Rosalie settled next to him on the sofa in their cozy house. Nothing had changed in the fenced-off district reserved for government officials. No protesters had breached the peaceful atmosphere, no debris littered the streets and certainly no corpses. "It was a very close call, though."

Norbert swiveled the vodka in its glass as if it were cognac. French liquor was hard to come by, even for the likes of him. "We were lucky. If we had waited until tomorrow before acting, it might have been too late."

"It wasn't luck, my dear. It was your swift and decisive action." Rosalie snuggled up against him and he wrapped his arm around her shoulders. As ever, he was grateful to have met her; she was the perfect wife and companion in every respect. Without her, he wouldn't have stayed in power all these years.

"Why didn't Otto Grotewohl's speech quell the unrest?" He wondered whether there might have been a way to get the situation under control without asking the Soviets for help. "We made a series of concessions. He expressly stated the withdrawal of the quota increases, promised a review of existing policies, public forums for grievances to be heard, and an investigation into alleged police brutality. We agreed to everything the strikers wanted, so why didn't they stop?"

"Because the uprising was the work of provocateurs and fascist agents of foreign powers as well as their accomplices from West German capitalist monopolies," Rosalie explained. Even before the Soviet military had been called on for help, the government had looked to find a culprit for the mass strikes. They'd found one in the class enemy and had dubbed the workers' strike "a fascist provocation by foreign agents".

"That's true." He cast her a knowing wink. Even in the intimacy of their own home, they would never admit the truth that their citizens were fed up with the socialist government and the majority would rather *vote with their feet* and leave the country for greener pastures in the West. It had been an issue long in coming, one that not even strict border controls had been able to stop.

He'd rather cling to the propagandistic fiction that the riot had been a fascist coup. The imperialist West was the perfect scapegoat to blame for the faults of his own government, so the absurd thesis, holding foreign agents responsible for the popular mass uprising, was going to be the new truth.

"It'll all work out fine, you'll see." Rosalie tried to cheer him up. "Otto called on all workers and honest citizens to help apprehend the provocateurs and hand them over to the state organizations. Before you know it, the Stasi will have arrested every last one of them. Then, our nation will run smoothly again."

"It's a shame we needed to call on the Soviets to finish the riots off. We should have been able to do it ourselves."

Rosalie put a hand on his arm, her eyes shining with love. "It wasn't your fault, darling. If anyone's, then I'd say Khrushchev and his New Course is to blame. When we were in Moscow you warned General Propov this wouldn't work, remember?"

"I do." Norbert suddenly felt tired. It was a Pyrrhic victory, obtained at the cost of losing control. The Soviets had declared martial law in East Berlin, thus officially resuming governmental power over the GDR. "If only we could prevent our citizens from listening to the damaging RIAS. Without their inciting broadcasts, nobody would have been alerted to the scattered strikes."

"West Berlin will always be a thorn in our side. Not even the attempt of our Soviet friends, to expel the Western Allies five years ago, was successful." Rosalie was referring to the Berlin Blockade, euphemistically called 'Traffic Controls' in official communications.

"How are we going to whip our nation back into shape?" Norbert tipped back his head, studying the ceiling as if the answers were written on there.

"The same way you always do it. Show understanding for the grievances of the people, while at the same time punishing everyone who insists on opposing."

Norbert looked down at her and smiled. "It's almost like having children, isn't it? Except that we have twenty million of them."

"You'd be a good father." Rosalie's eyes held a hint of sadness. Having their own children was the one thing they had never been able to achieve.

"And you a good mother." After holding her hand for a few minutes, new energy surged within and he said, "Tomorrow, I'll arrange for a press conference to calm the masses. I'll be committing to change and social harmony."

"Meanwhile, behind closed doors, you'll work tirelessly to neutralize the people who led the strikes. Ringleaders, key activists, union leaders, advocates for free speech, they will all be arrested and used as horrible examples to deter the nation from seeing these atrocious men and women as heroes." Rosalie clapped her hands with delight. Her penchant for cruel punishments was both endearing and appalling.

After a minute of silence during which he emptied his glass of vodka, he voiced the concern lurking in the back of his mind. "I'm worried about our friend, Vladimir. He seemed a bit too eager to let the strikes continue."

"I noticed the same." Rosalie had been present throughout the government meetings in case a translator was needed, although she always refrained from voicing an opinion in public.

"It's not his usual behavior to be lenient. All that talk of peaceful protests and the workers only wanting better living conditions. Where would we be if we gave everyone what their hearts desired? Back into chaos, or worse, the Nazi's fascist reign." Norbert was talking himself into a rage. He considered Vladi's hesitation to deploy the Soviet military as a betrayal of duty to both mother Russia and the German government.

"Love makes a man forget himself," Rosalie stated with a laugh.

"Love? What are you talking about, dearest?" Norbert counted on his wife to keep him abreast of petty gossip. Often, the irrelevant actions of a powerful man could be used to initiate the downfall of an onerous rival. Thus, he kept a dossier about the government officials, and the Stasi kept many, many dossiers about almost anyone in the country.

"It seems our Vladi is madly in love and his affliction has addled his brains." Rosalie poured both of them a new glass, before she added, "She's a common German woman, no less. Her name is Floriane Eilers, she works in a chocolate factory and, despite being a party member, she's never volunteered for a political activity."

"You have done your homework." Norbert smiled.

"I was going to tell you about it later, since I didn't want to spoil the celebratory mood after wangling back our nation from the abyss of the imperialist instigators."

Norbert appreciated her attempt to keep unpleasant facts away from him at least for a few hours. Nonetheless, he shrugged. "I guess it's too late for that, so what else did you dig up about our Russian friend?"

"I always pegged Vladi as far too ambitious to let personal affection hinder his progress. It appears I was wrong." Her eyes twinkled with delight, which told Norbert she had a great story to relate.

"You're making me curious," he indulged her.

"His little sweetheart was arrested during the protests."

"Serendipity, indeed. I dare say a period of separation may serve as a catalyst to restore his senses," Norbert chuckled.

"Ha! You don't yet know the half of it! It gets much better."

Now Norbert was seriously intrigued. "What happened next, my love?"

"She was released from prison this morning, on account of a Soviet officer intervening on her behalf."

Norbert didn't ask how Rosalie had received this crucial information in such a timely manner. She had informers everywhere, securing their collaboration with a mixture of generous gifts and well-placed threats. It worked exceedingly well, since nobody wanted to cross the wife of the most powerful man in the state.

"That Soviet officer, I imagine, was none other than our Vladi?"

"You're such a clever man, which is the reason I love you so much." She kissed him on the lips, making him forget Vladi's crimes for a few minutes.

When they finally came up for air, he said, "What are we going to do with him?"

"That's entirely up to you." She smiled. "You could deliver him on a silver plate to Semyonov or the Kremlin...or use the knowledge to your own advantage."

"I love your way of thinking." He grinned at her. "Perhaps we should put him under surveillance. What do you think?"

Rosalie's face lit up. "I knew you would suggest this, so I've taken the liberty of having a word with his driver, Axel Becker, and instructed him not to let Vladi out of his sight."

"I love you so much, sweetheart."

CHAPTER 30

S omething was off.

Vladi had been tied down in official meetings, dealing with the aftermath of the riots all day. On the surface, everything seemed to be as usual, yet he couldn't shake off an uneasy feeling.

Years of training in the Red Army Intelligence had given him a sixth and seventh sense for danger. Today, it screamed at him from all sides. Used to getting to the source quickly, it irked him that he found no clue. Not in the behavior of the people he dealt with, not in carelessly dropped words, not even in surreptitious gazes behind his back.

After hours of puzzling over the reason for his anxiety he chalked it up to the quelled riots and his worry about Flori. He'd expected at least some gratitude from her, instead she'd been infuriated. Deep down in his heart, he understood her reaction, yet it angered him that she refused to put herself in his shoes.

If he'd told her his true identity, she would never have entertained the idea of going out with him. Couldn't she understand that?

Deep in thought, he was caught unawares when his chauffeur walked toward him. "Are you ready to go home?"

"Can you drop me off at the Tiergarten? I need to breathe some fresh air and clear my head." Vladi had planned to pass by Floriane's from there, which Axel didn't need to know about.

"I certainly can." Axel escorted him to the car, of the same make as the one Vladi had *borrowed* the day before to liberate Floriane from jail.

When they arrived at the Tiergarten, Axel said, "I'll wait here for you."

"That won't be necessary, I can walk to my accommodation." Under no circumstances did Vladi want the driver anywhere near Flori.

"I'm very sorry, but I'll need to drive you home. One of the measures implemented with the martial law is to avoid all potential threat."

"Don't you think I can fend for myself?" Vladi pointed toward his trusted Tokarev pistol in its holster.

"I have no doubt about that. But orders are orders." Axel gave a shrug of apology.

Vladi groaned. "Well, I guess you can walk with me for a while and then drive me to Karlshorst. Would that work?"

"Certainly, comrade."

Inwardly, Vladi cursed the precautionary measure, which might be necessary to protect people like Gentner or Grotewohl from harm, but not a fully trained agent like himself. Maintaining a brisk pace, he strode through the park, pondering the best way to lose Axel and visit Floriane.

In theory, he could simply ask the chauffeur to drive him to her building. However, the unease he'd sensed all day warned him not to draw attention to their relationship. His intervention to get her out of prison compromised them both and the last thing he wanted was for her to be arrested again.

"Will you be recalled to Moscow now that the SCC has taken over governmental control?" Axel asked jovially.

Vladi wasn't willing to discuss political issues, aware that loose lips could sink ships. "I have not received my orders yet. You'll be among the first to be officially notified."

Axel shrugged. "To me, it's all the same, I will serve whoever I'm assigned to."

"For now, I'd like to return to Karlshorst, there's plenty of paperwork waiting for me."

"With pleasure. I'll be waiting for you outside the house in case you need me."

"That won't be necessary, since I fully expect to be drowned in work." Vladi wrinkled his nose. "Writing the reports always takes hours."

"In any case, I'll be there until curfew." Axel opened the passenger door for Vladi, before he walked around the vehicle to install himself behind the wheel. It wasn't long before the vehicle stopped in front of Vladi's lodgings. "I must remind you the curfew is strictly enforced, even for men in uniform, except if you have a special permit."

"Thanks for reminding me. As I said, I won't be going anywhere." Inwardly, Vladi seethed. Did Axel genuinely believe a simple curfew would deter him? "Goodnight."

He walked into the house, to see Captain Zhukov sitting in the living room, reading the *Prawda* newspaper.

"Good evening, comrade." Vladi had hoped not to find Zhukov home, so as to make his plan of sneaking out a lot easier. Apparently, fate had conspired against him visiting Flori tonight. He chuckled to himself; much tougher obstacles would be needed to keep him from seeing her.

"Good evening," Zhukov replied. "Have you seen the news?"

"Unfortunately not. I was tied up in meetings all day."

"The fascist agitators almost burned down the country with their riots," Zhukov said.

Although that statement was grossly exaggerated propaganda, Vladi kept his face serene. "It was a good thing our military squashed the protests so quickly."

"I hear the German government arrested at least ten thousand fascist rabble rousers last night." Zhukov put his newspaper aside.

"They need to do away with the troublemakers, or there'll be another riot at some point in the future." Vladi repeated the official wording without believing a word of it. Sensing that Zhukov was up for a chat, he preempted, "You'll have to excuse me, I need to write my reports for Moscow."

"Perhaps we could have a drink later this evening? To celebrate the successful defeat of the fascist riot?"

It would have been downright rude to deny the invitation, so he nodded his agreement. It was looking as if he wouldn't be able to sneak out to visit Floriane tonight, unless he wanted to raise suspicions.

The next morning, he set his alarm early and got up despite the awful hangover caused by too much vodka. Zhukov had been hell-bent on getting Vladi drunk. However, he had merely succeeded in passing out himself. Vladi chuckled at the memory of dragging the unconscious man into his room.

By then, it had been way past midnight, so there was no point in swinging by Floriane's, who'd be fast asleep at such a late hour.

Downing two glasses of water to combat the lingering headache, he peeked through the curtains in the kitchen, to see Axel's car waiting in front. So the driver was serious in his quest to protect Vladi from imagined harm.

He walked to Zhukov's room, listening to the dreadful snores, which even the door between them couldn't muffle, and left the house through the back door. Well before six a.m. it was already light and he congratulated himself for his choice of dressing in civilian clothes, since they would make it so much easier to go unnoticed.

He waved at Floriane, who left the building at the same time he arrived in front.

"You have some nerve coming to see me now!" she lashed out. "How dare you show your face after standing me up last night?"

"I'm so sorry, darling," he replied, presenting a picture of absolute sorrow and dejection. "I couldn't keep my promise as it would have threatened your safety."

Her pursed lips softened a tiny bit, yet he read in her expression that she wasn't mollified yet.

"So you stood me up to protect me? Just like you lied to me for my own good?"

"I would lie a hundred times just to be near you." Vladi was an expert with the ladies and knew how to convince a woman that he was sincere. "My need to see you, to be near you, has driven me to do things I wouldn't normally do."

"Oh, stop that." She swatted at him and he realized he'd almost won her over. A bit more groveling and she'd be putty in his hands.

"Your wish is my command." Not waiting for a reply, he added, "May I accompany you to the factory? I urgently need to talk with you."

"If it's so urgent, why not?" Her nonchalant tone didn't fool Vladi. He acknowledged how much yesterday's arrest still rattled her.

He yearned to wrap her in his arms and whisper sweet words of assurance into her ear, promising to keep her safe from every peril – perceived or real. He resisted, because meanwhile he knew her well enough to realize this would be the wrong approach.

"Thank you for allowing me to explain things to you, Floriane," he began. "I hope you can someday find it in your heart to forgive me."

"Perhaps we could start over?" Her eyes were filled with the same strong affection he felt for her.

"First, there's something important I need to discuss with you." He pondered how to best broach the delicate topic. "The government has plans to punish everyone involved in the riots."

"They'll be quite busy doing so, there were thousands of us." She waved his remark away. "Furthermore, Max Fechner, the minister of justice, has assured via radio that strikes aren't a crime in a socialist country and nobody has to fear persecution for participating in them."

Vladi bit on his lips. He wasn't allowed to tell her that Fechner had made himself a persona non grata with these assertions and was going to be arrested for his crimes against the nation. "I heard his interview too, and am as optimistic as you are. This doesn't change the fact that I discovered your name on a list of ringleaders up for arrest."

"They already did that, remember? You freed me." Floriane simply was too inexperienced in politics to understand the gravity of the situation. If the Stasi was on to her, Vladi's influence wouldn't save her a second time.

"The authorities might come for you at any moment. If that happens, I won't be able to help, don't you see that?" he pleaded with her.

"No one is going to be prosecuted for their participation in the protests. Reforms have been announced. Things are going to get better. Why should I leave when there's hope on the horizon? Furthermore, I've done nothing wrong."

Her nonchalance made him want to scream.

"However, that's not always enough. Please, hear me out, will you?"

Floriane stopped to look at him. "If it eases your mind."

"It does." If he weren't so occupied trying to whip some sense into her, he'd kiss her breathless. The memory of their time in bed shot hot into his loins, causing him to lose his train of thought for a few seconds. "Look...I don't want anything bad to happen to you. I can't prove it, nor do I have substantiated facts; what I'm going to say is based purely on a hunch. But in my decades with the inte... the military, my intuition has never led me astray. On the contrary, it has saved my life at least a dozen times."

"Alright, tell me what you're so worried about." Finally, a flicker of understanding seemed to reach her brain.

"I have a very bad feeling the government is going to arrest all the ringleaders and make an example of them."

"I'm hardly a ringleader. Max was." Her face spoke of horrible grief and he wanted again to wrap her up in his arms. Instead, he pressed his point.

"The GDR leadership quashed the riots, now they want to eradicate the protesters."

"Your tanks mowed down our people." She glared at him with animosity, pressing her lips into a thin line.

"Because your government asked us to. I was there." He omitted that he'd been the one to effectually issue the order.

"Alright, if what you say is true, and I'm indeed on some kind of black list, what do you suggest I should do?"

"You must leave the country." He stopped and placed a hand on her shoulder, his worry for her almost killing him.

Floriane sighed dramatically. "Don't you think that's a bit extreme?"

"Not at all. If you had been in this business as long as I have, you wouldn't be so cavalier about it." He put all the weight of his conviction into his gaze, willing her to take the danger seriously.

"I...I've never contemplated defecting to the west. I mean, I like it here. My sister is here, Max..." Her face fell at the mention of her late friend. "My friends, my workplace, my apartment, my home, my everything."

"Your reluctance is understandable." He inched nearer to her, wanting her to feel his love. "But you might lose all of it anyway if you're given a long prison sentence, or worse..." He let the threat linger in the air, to force her to accept the gravity of her situation.

"I'll think about it," she agreed, as they reached the underground station where she'd catch her train to work.

"Please do. I'll pick you up from work this afternoon." Under no circumstances, did he want her to go home alone, since he strongly feared she might be arrested. At least with him by her side, he'd be able to prevent that.

"Thank you." A smile appeared on her beautiful face and she gave him a passionate kiss, which ended much too soon with the arrival of her train.

I love you, he whispered, as he stared at her vanishing back. Then he returned to his lodgings, musing over the irony of finally finding a woman he loved with all his heart, only to be forced to send her away.

CHAPTER 31

F lori arrived at work with no time to spare. She was hurriedly changing into the work uniform when Klara rushed inside, late as always.

"Have you already heard?" she yelled into the locker room.

"Spare your gossip for the break, or Herr Schmidt will unleash his wrath on us," Helga admonished her.

"He won't be able to." Klara's smirk faded as quickly as it had appeared.

"Oh, come on, what's your excuse this time?"

Klara swallowed visibly and flopped down on the bench in front of her locker. "He's been arrested."

"What?" Half a dozen heads whipped around in unison.

"Is this some kind of sick joke?" Carolin asked.

"No." Klara's snow-white face was evidence enough that she wasn't in a joking mood.

"Are you sure? Maybe it was a misunderstanding? Tell us what happened?" The women bombarded her with questions.

Klara shook her head, burying in her hands, until she raised her gaze to look at her colleagues. "What if they come for us too?"

"Why should they? We have done nothing wrong," Flori soothed her friend, despite icy shivers trickling down her spine.

"Herr Schmidt was a one-hundred-fifty-percent communist, a faithful party member, always toeing the line," Klara said between sobs.

"Why would they arrest him then?" Carolin asked, even though all of them suspected it was to do with the mass strike.

"I don't understand..." Helga mumbled. "He advocated against a strike, claiming it would hurt the economy and thus ourselves. He only joined us that day, because everyone else went. When he saw the thousands of workers marching, he couldn't believe it at first."

Flori kept silent, her mind swimming with images of her own arrest, the night spent in prison, the humiliation experienced during the pat down. Her inner turmoil was so powerful, she had to stabilize herself by placing one hand against the smooth, cold metal of the locker door.

"Are you alright?" Helga squinted her eyes in concern.

"Yes. Just a bit faint, must be the stress." Flori hadn't told anyone about her time in prison and her rescue by Vladi. Instead, she'd excused her absence with a summer cold, caught due to the incessant rain on the day of the strike.

"You aren't pregnant, are you?" Helga, mother of four, scrutinized her.

"No. Certainly not." Vladi had taken precautions by using a condom and, in any case, their lovemaking had been much too recent to result in morning sickness. Thinking of Vladi gave her renewed energy, along with the harsh realization that he was right. Her life *was* in danger.

If the Stasi could arrest a faithful party member such as Herr Schmidt, then nobody was out of reach. Whether her name actually was on a black list, or Vladi had invented it to emphasize his point, didn't make any difference. She wasn't going to risk being thrown into jail a second time.

"You look awful, shall I bring you a glass of water?" Helga persisted.

"That would be nice, thank you." While Flori was waiting for the water, she decided it was best to leave the factory right away to return home and pack a few things. Since illegally leaving the country was punished with up to five years of prison time, she would have to be extremely careful about it.

As soon as Helga returned with the glass in hand, Flori made a suffering grimace and said, "You're right, I'm not feeling well. Would you please advise the personnel department that I'm still sick with my summer flu?"

"Do you want me to accompany you home?"

"No thanks," Flori answered in a meek voice. "I guess I'll manage."

"Promise to go to bed and keep yourself warm? And drink hot milk with honey, it works wonders on a cold."

"I will." Suddenly, she couldn't leave the factory fast enough, imagining Stasi members lurking in every corner ready to pounce on her. In a rush of emotion, she wrapped her arms around Helga's neck. "Thank you so much."

"Come on. It's just a cold, you're not going to die." Helga cast her a slightly bemused glance.

The siren announcing the beginning of their shift thankfully meant there was no time to exchange further words, or Flori would have blurted out her plan to escape.

"Get better," Carolin said.

"See you soon," Klara added.

And then her friends were gone. Flori became acutely aware that this was the first of many spoken and unspoken goodbyes. Once she'd slipped across the border into the Western sectors there was no way to return – ever.

A flash of panic seared through her body. *Katja.* What would become of her little sister? As soon as she was out of sight of the factory, she hastened toward the underground station, driven by the urgent need to get away.

Back at home, Katja started when she noticed Flori standing in the doorway..

"What on earth are you doing here? Shouldn't you..." Katja left her sentence unfinished as she became aware of Flori's agitated condition. "Has something happened?"

"I must leave," Flori said.

"I thought you'd left a while ago. You are going to be late for work."

Flori violently shook her head. "No, you don't understand. I must leave the country. Now."

"Why?" Understanding settled on Katja's features. "Does it have anything to do with your arrest?"

"Yes. No. I mean, I'm not sure." Flori was a muddled mess, unable to form a coherent sentence. "Vladi says—"

"So you've forgiven him?"

"Not entirely. In any case, my arrest wasn't his fault. On the contrary, he freed me from prison."

"Are you sure you can trust him? This could be a trap to facilitate another arrest."

Flori stared at her sister. "The Stasi doesn't need traps, they can abscond people without a reason. And weren't you the one who told me that Vladi risked a lot to save me and thus must truly love me?"

Katja worried her lip. "I did. I'm having second thoughts. How well do you know him?"

"Not that well," Flori said lamely. Indeed, Vladi kept so many secrets from her, such as what exactly his role was in the Red Army and why he'd been deployed to Berlin. Torn between her love for Vladi and the weight of Katja's words, she explained, "It's hard to explain, but I'm one-hundred-percent sure that he truly cares for me and wants to protect me. He was adamant that I'm in danger if I choose to stay in the country."

"So, you're leaving everything behind, even me?" Katja's eyes filled with sadness.

"You have university waiting for you come fall. I can't expect you to throw your future away for me. Your freedom is not at risk."

Katja rolled her eyes. "Sometimes I wonder how you can be so naïve. Don't you know what happens to the relatives of those who have fled the republic?"

Flori's shoulders sagged. How could she leave her beloved sister behind, all alone in a country ripped apart by turmoil? In her anguish she hadn't considered the repercussions. Most likely, Katja would be interrogated by the Stasi and her university admission would be revoked on the grounds of being politically unreliable.

"I'm coming with you," Katja stated matter-of-factly.

"But how?"

"Together we'll find a way."

"We better start planning then." Flori settled on the sofa, looking around the apartment at the few things they owned.

"We can't take much or we'll raise suspicion." Katja's gaze followed Flori's, until it paused on a photograph of the two sisters with Max. It had been taken a year ago, on a trip to one of the nearby lakes. "I miss him so much."

"I do, too. He was so much more than just a friend for me. He was my pillar of strength after our parents died. He always encouraged me when I was overwhelmed by the difficulties of raising you while eking out a living for us. Without him, I would have given up more than once." Tears pooled in her eyes, and she looked down at the floor, so Katja wouldn't see them. "Max loved you so much."

"And I loved him," Katja sobbed.

Vladi arrived that evening to find the sisters sitting on packed suitcases, or rather on an unpretentious backpack each.

"We're ready to leave." Flori pointed to the luggage, each filled with a set of spare clothes, along with their dearest things: the picture of Max, a few reminders of their parents and a lot of optimism.

"You can't just up and leave." He didn't seem comfortable with her decision.

His sudden objection confused her. "It was you, who told me of the danger here."

"Sweet Floriane, you need a better plan than to simply walk away. Due to the riots, they've closed the sector borders. It might be days or even weeks before anyone without a permit can cross into the Western sectors again." His explanation washed over her like a wave of cold water.

"Is this some kind of trick?" Katja narrowed her eyes at him.

"No. It's the truth."

"So, how do you suggest we escape?" Katja challenged him.

"I'll organize a permit for you, but you can't cross tonight, it has to be in the morning, pretending you're en route to work." When Vladi's eyes locked with hers, she saw a deep yearning in them, which completely melted her heart. With her stomach doing somersaults, she did her best to keep a sensual tremble from her voice when she answered with her assent.

Katja seemed to sense her sister's need to be alone with the man she loved, because she said, "I want to go over to Max's place to say goodbye."

Flori embraced her, staying silent for several seconds, until Katja whispered into her ear, "Don't worry about me, I'll sleep at Max's place and won't return before dawn."

"Thank you." A sliver of guilt pierced Flori, because she thought about making love with Vladi, when her sister was so obviously heartbroken.

CHAPTER 32

Vladi woke in the wee hours of the morning with Floriane snuggled up in his arms. Their night together had been the most exquisite experience, and once again he was astonished at the intensity of the feelings he harbored for this woman.

With her by his side, time seemed to stand still. The troubles surrounding them faded into oblivion when they touched. His heart ached at having to let her go. Even after knowing her for such a short time, she'd ingrained herself into his heart and soul, never to be forgotten, however long he lived.

She stretched her slender limbs as she awoke, the smile on her face a feast of love.

"Did you sleep well?" he asked softly.

"Very well, although I much preferred what we did before I fell asleep." The mischievous grin shot heat straight into his loins.

Unfortunately, there was no time for a repeat, since he needed to organize permits for her and Katja for their travel to West Berlin. He winced as the thought stabbed his heart with a pain as sharp and real as a physical wound.

"Are you hurt?" Floriane's face crunched in worry.

"No, my love. Merely sad to leave you."

Apparently considering the consequences of her escape to the

West for the first time, she flinched. "I don't want to lose you. I love you."

"I love you too, my darling. More than I have ever loved anyone." Try as he might to banish the painful thought of their parting, it settled deep in his bones, every cell in his body aching for her.

"Come with me," Flori begged. "I can't bear the thought of never seeing you again."

He caressed her dear face. "It's not so easy."

Vladi had toyed with the idea of absconding every once in a while, without ever giving it serious consideration. It had been a tantrum he'd thrown when another stupidity or atrocity crossed his path – like the mowing down of peaceful protests with tanks.

Last night, everything had changed. In Floriane's arms he'd found a bliss never known before. It was as if he'd waited for her all his life, to finally be complete.

A smile stole across his face and he hugged her tighter against him, letting his hand wander down her naked back. His heart ached with an astonishing intensity, as if already missing her presence.

"Together we can make it work." Her expectant gaze rested on him.

A million notions raced through his mind. Was he prepared to give up everything for the woman he loved? His career, his life in Moscow, his friends, his family? Was he willing to betray his motherland, the socialist ideals he'd internalized, just to be with her?

"For you and Katja, it's easy to escape. You're German citizens. If I want to defect, it will need much more complicated preparation."

"Why can't you come with us? We'll figure it out once we are there."

He chuckled at her naivety. "Oh my darling. That's not how it works. I'm a Soviet citizen, a high-ranking member of the military. The West will only accept me if I give them valuable information in exchange. Otherwise, they'll throw me into jail under suspicion of being a spy – or simply send me back. I'm not exactly keen on either of these options."

"Others have done it, so it's possible," she protested.

It was true, there were some prominent dissidents like Werner Böhm, Norbert Gentner's right hand, shortly after the war or the NKVD officer, Viktor Kravchenko.

"Organizing my own escape will take time and effort."

"Please promise you'll at least try." There was so much love in her gaze, it was impossible for him to ignore her wish.

Pressing kisses on her shoulder, he took his sweet time to ponder his options. Then he looked into her eyes again, his heart filling with the need to share the rest of his life with this wonderful woman.

"I promise. As soon as you've safely crossed to West Berlin and have been flown out to the Western zones, I'll begin my preparation. But it might take several months and most probably I won't be able to contact you, in order not to jeopardize my defection."

"That's all I need to know." She snuggled up against him and they made love in a quick and frantic fashion, clinging to each other like castaways gripping a log to keep afloat.

Just as he leapt from the bed to get dressed, he heard the key in the door turn. Katja was back. It took him a full three seconds to slip into his pants and shirt, before he stepped out into the living room, greeting her with, "Good morning, Katja. Ready to go to work?"

She nodded calmly.

"I'll meet you and Floriane in one hour at Friedrichstrasse." And with these words he walked out.

CHAPTER 33

"Are you sure Vladi will come through with the permits?" Katja asked for the hundredth time as they walked toward Friedrichstrasse, which was the last station in East Berlin before the underground line crossed the border into the British sector.

In recent years, it had become the main hub for illegal departures from the GDR for the cost of twenty pfennig, the price of a ticket to the first western station, Lehrter Stadtbahnhof. The government knew about this loophole to freedom and had installed several watch and control towers along the platforms.

Since many East Berliners worked in the West, and vice versa, it was usually no problem to cross, as long as one didn't carry a suitcase or bulky pack, which might arouse suspicion.

Following the strikes though, the borders had been closed except to citizens who provided an employment paper, or similar, in one of the Western sectors.

"Don't worry. He won't leave us out to dry." After last night, Flori implicitly trusted him.

"How do you know? He could be a Romeo agent."

Reeling from the implied insult, Flori lashed out. "Stop that already. You've read far too many espionage thrillers."

"It's not unusual for the class enemy to employ such tactics."

Flori stopped to look at her sister, who was worrying her lip. "I get that you are nervous. But please stop talking such nonsense. He's not the class enemy, neither are we. We are supposed to be on the same side. And why would he try to get us out if he were trying to spy on me?"

"I'm sorry." Guilt flashed through Katja's eyes. "I guess I'm just anxious."

"You need to stop. I mean it. Anyone with half a brain can see you're up to something sinister from a mile away. If you don't calm down, the border guards will pick us out for sure." Flori was anxious herself, since so much could go wrong.

"I know." Katja groaned. "It's scary how much our lives have changed within a few days, isn't it?"

Flori could only nod at the truth of her sister's words. She didn't have the heart to tell her that a lot more was going to change. As soon as they stepped into the temporary reception center in Marienfeld, they were officially refugees without a home, a job, money, or basically anything.

"There he is." Flori waved at Vladi, who was walking toward them. His face was as smooth as ever, although when he came nearer she sensed his tension. "Hello Vladi."

"Good morning, ladies." His smile eased his stiff expression. "I've got you both permissions to cross the border to your workplace as seamstresses in a clothing factory."

"I'd love to work there for real," Flori giggled, which earned her a stern gaze.

"Don't joke about this. You must be absolutely confident when crossing the border. If the guards have even the slightest doubt, they'll pick you out to interrogate you." His voice softened. "The papers are genuine, so this shouldn't present a problem. Still, the guards can prevent you from crossing if they see fit. It's considered unpatriotic to work in the West sector."

"It's also—" Katja stopped mid-sentence at an elbow nudge from Flori, who didn't want to risk offending Vladi by whatever snide remark her sister was going to make.

"Thank you so much." She didn't dare touch Vladi in public, afraid someone might be watching them and figure out their illegal plans. It was frightening and exhilarating at the same time.

He took her aside and said, "It would be suspicious if I came with you, so you'll be on your own. Once you're in the West, we won't be able to communicate anymore. Send a postcard to a few of your coworkers, then the word will get around."

"How am I going to hear about you?" Her breath hitched in her breast. She hadn't considered being cut off from any and all information about her previous life and especially about Vladi. "What if you have to go back to Moscow for a while?"

"Oh my love." His face fell. „I'm afraid there's nothing you can do but wait. If I'm not to jeopardize my defection I can't do anything out of the usual, especially not contacting a person in the West. You'll have to have faith. I promise that I will do everything in my power to join you as soon as I can."

"But how will you know where I am?" The lump forming in her throat barely allowed her to croak out the words.

"Do you know anyone, whom I might contact?"

"Not really...or yes. My coworker, Else, she moved in with her cousin Marlene Kupfer a few months ago." She pulled out a piece of paper and scribbled Marlene's address on it, handing it over to Vladi.

"Marlene Kupfer...wasn't she in the bar the night we met?"

"Yes, that was her."

"I think we've met before. She was Werner Böhm's girlfriend, wasn't she?"

"Who is Werner Böhm?" Flori asked.

"Never mind." Vladi grinned. "A former acquaintance. He defected to the West five years ago, works in Wiesbaden at the American radio station now. I was convinced Marlene had followed him; the two of them were madly in love."

An icy hand squeezed her heart, as realization dawned that Marlene and Werner had been in a similar situation five years ago – and they hadn't found a happily ever after.

Vladi seemed to have read her mind, because he said, "Their

situation was different. He didn't defect because of her, I believe. And they might have decided they didn't fit together after all."

"Don't make me wait too long, I'm already missing you," Flori pleaded.

"We should really get going," Katja interrupted. "Or we'll be late for work."

Vladi chuckled. "Yes, best to cross with the morning rush of workers." Then he pressed a quick kiss on Flori's lips. "I love you."

Almost immobilized by grief, Flori somehow managed to walk beside her sister, who dragged her away from the man she loved. They arrived at the platform without incident. From there she was able to look down onto the street beneath them, where she spotted Vladi looking up. For a fleeting second their eyes met. Then the train entered the station and she stepped on board and into freedom.

"I'll wait for you, however long it takes." In the depths of her sorrow, Flori sent positive energy toward the man she loved so much, acknowledging that their souls would forever remain entwined, even during their forced separation.

LETTER FROM MARION

Dear Reader,

Thank you so much for reading *Against the Odds*. I'd been toying with writing a book about Vladi for quite a while, but had gotten sidetracked with my other series *Margarete's Journey* and *The German Wives*.

You may know that in West Germany, the 17th of June used to be *Tag der Deutschen Einheit,* day of German unity. It was made our national holiday, following the quashed uprising in the GDR, as a reminder of the people's desire for freedom and one united nation.

The workers' uprising in 1953 was the perfect backdrop for the fifth book in the *Berlin Fractured* series, and who other than Vladi, our most beloved villain, could be the protagonist? I wanted to uproot his deepest convictions and truly get him into inner conflicts. Thus, Floriane showed up.

She represents many GDR citizens at that time: war-tired, eking out a modest living, hoping for a better future and willing to work hard for it. People like her and Max were not, per se, opposed to socialism, since they realized it had many positive characteristics, such as free school education.

Over the years, a huge part of the population became disillusioned with the political elites, who corrupted the system for their own benefit or to fulfil directives from Moscow. Since dissenting opinions were silenced through strict measures, millions of people – in total almost 20% of the population – "voted with their feet" and fled to West Germany, where they had not only the chance for a better economic situation, but also the freedom of speech, religion, and press.

That exit route was gradually made more difficult by the building of a 1300 km (900 miles) death strip along the inner-German border. Fleeing the country was rendered all but impossible with the construction of the 160 km (100 miles) wall around West Berlin.

My son and I recently undertook a bike tour along the *Mauerweg*, a newly installed bike route closely following the former wall. If you ever visit Berlin, I recommend hiking or biking at least a part of the round tour.

It has informative and emotional orange signposts, depicting short biographies of the victims who lost their lives at, or nearby, the wall while trying to escape a tyrannical regime. A special highlight for us was the former watch tower in Niederneuendorf, which has been converted into a museum.

Perhaps you remember that the Niederneuendorfer lake was the location of Victor's accident in book 4 **Into the Unkown**.

Anyway, back to this book

The governing SED party led a fierce battle against the church and especially against the Junge Gemeinde, which wasn't a formal organisation (because that was forbidden), but a form of Protestant community work. The SED repeatedly urged young Christians to join the official FDJ and work for peace and friendship among nations within the national youth organization The reason was, patently, to have better control over young Christians and to subject them to ideological indoctrination.

When visiting Delitzsch, a town near Leipzig, in early 2023, I chanced upon the Böhme chocolate factory. A huge sign on the building wall said it had been founded in 1894. At that time (not in 1894, mind you!) I was writing the outline for **Against the Odds** and decided on the spot that Floriane would work in a chocolate factory.

Following this decision, I needed to do plenty of research regarding the chocolate making process, small parts of it making it into the book. The practical research of tasting different products, was especially pleasurable. ☺

I never ate Vitalade, though, the ubiquitous chocolate substitute in the GDR. Soon after the German reunification in 1989, when cocoa was not a scarcity anymore, its production was stopped.

Norbert Gentner's role is modelled on Walter Ulbricht, who was the second man in the GDR for many years, although Norbert's personal life with Rosalie is completely fictional.

Stalin's death brought plenty of change to Soviet politics, among them the *New Course*, which saw a relaxation of ideological standards, the supposed end of terror, and a focus on production of consumer goods instead of heavy industry. The easing of persecution for dissenting opinions became the kindling for the mass protests.

I have tried to follow the real events and their time schedule as closely as possible. As for the anecdotes sprinkled into the story (i.e. the mayor in the cesspit, the student crushed by the tank), all of them happened in real life, even though I have changed the exact location or time.

Vladi is the combination of several roles and individuals, who all worked together to quash the uprising with the help of Soviet tanks. Years later, the same happened in Hungary (1956) and Czechoslovakia (1968).

Contrary to SED propaganda, the American RIAS radio station never intended to incite the protests. It became the catalyst of the uprising without wanting to, due to the mere fact that they reported on it. The station broadcasted the strikes nationwide - whereas GDR radio kept silent about them - thus giving the workers the knowledge about others in the same situation.

If you've been rooting for a happy end for Vladi and Floriane, I can tell you this much: after some ordeals (which may or may not make it into another book) Vladi manages to escape to West Germany and is then reunited with Floriane, to live happily ever after.

Katja studies engineering at the Technical University in Aachen, where she meets a very nice young man, whom she later marries, although she'll never forget her first love, Max.

And if you're wondering about Vladi's backstory with Marlene Kupfer and Zara Ulbert, you might want to read the previous books in the series.

Start with **From the Ashes.**

Thank you again so much for reading **Against the Odds**. If you liked it I would appreciate a sincere review on the retailer of your choice.

Sign up for my reader group to receive exclusive background information and be the first one to know when a new book is released.

https://kummerow.info/

Marion Kummerow

ALSO BY MARION KUMMEROW

Love and Resistance in WW2 Germany

Unrelenting

Unyielding

Unwavering

War Girl Series

Downed over Germany (Prequel)

Blonde Angel: War Girl Ursula (Book 1)

War Girl Lotte (Book 2)

War Girl Anna (Book 3)

Reluctant Informer (Book 4)

Trouble Brewing (Book 5)

Fatal Encounter (Book 6)

Uncommon Sacrifice (Book 7)

Bitter Tears (Book 8)

Secrets Revealed (Book 9)

Together at Last (Book 10)

Endless Ordeal (Book 11)

Not Without My Sister (Spin-off)

Second Chance at First Love (romantic spin-off)

Berlin Fractured

From the Ashes (Book 1)

On the Brink (Book 2)

In the Skies (Book 3)

Into the Unknown (Book 4)

Against the Odds (Book 5)

Margarete's Story

Turning Point (Prequel)

A Light in the Window

From the Dark We Rise

The Girl in the Shadows

Daughter of the Dawn

Standalone

The Orphan's Mother

German Wives

The Berlin Wife

The Berlin Wife's Choice

The Berlin Wife's Resistance

Find all my books here:

http://www.kummerow.info

CONTACT ME

I truly appreciate you taking the time to read (and enjoy) my books.
And I'd be thrilled to hear from you!
If you'd like to get in touch with me you can do so via

Facebook:
http://www.facebook.com/AutorinKummerow

Website
http://www.kummerow.info

Printed in Great Britain
by Amazon

39848589R00128